# GETAWAY BAY

GETAWAY BAY® RESORT ROMANCE, BOOK 2

## ELANA JOHNSON

ISBN-13: 978-1-63876-011-5

# ONE

ESTHER PINNETT GROANED as she rolled over and silenced her alarm. At least it wasn't dark despite the earliness of the hour. She should be used to getting up by five o'clock, but it still seemed like a chore every morning.

She sat up, the tropical breeze coming through the open window only a hint of the storm that was coming toward the island. Sighing, she got herself into the shower, choosing to use her purple shampoo that morning, along with a blonditioner that was supposed to make her highlights brighter.

So she'd been coloring her hair for a few years. It was still naturally blonde, but every once in a while, everyone needed a bit of help. Esther took hers in the form of coffee with caramel and cream, and hair dye. It wasn't a crime.

She brushed her teeth, put magnesium oil on her softer upper arms, and went through her hair routine with the creams and gels and dusts.

Esther thrived on routine. Lived for it. Stepped into her neatly pressed black slacks and paired them with a blue, white, and black flowery blouse, exactly the same way she did every morning. Just before she left her bungalow for the day, she'd put on her black suit jacket, all she ever wore on the island, rain or shine.

True, she didn't drive every day, but her first client of the morning did sometimes work seven days a week. And it was seven days a week of torture, because her first client of the day was Marshall Robison.

Tall Marshall, with dark-haired, black sand-colored eyes, and the richest man in the islands. And the man Esther had had a secret crush on for two years.

Two very long years.

Over seven hundred days of torture, driving him from his cliff-side mansion to his offices at the Robison Plantation, the largest conglomerate of pineapple plantations in the islands. Sometimes she drove him to the beach. Or to his favorite restaurants. Or to his best friend's hotel, Sweet Breeze, right on Getaway Bay.

He also went to multiple company functions, each with a different woman on his arm. Esther had started giving those jobs to someone else, as she could hardly stand to be in the car with him and his giggly girlfriend-for-the-night.

She knew how he took his coffee, that he did a crossword puzzle every single day, and that his birthday was coming up in just a couple of days. She also knew she wanted more than one date with the man who didn't go on second dates. She wasn't sure what that made her, other than delusional.

*Hopeful*, she told herself. *Optimistic.*

After she'd brushed her teeth, slipped into heels, and applied her makeup—in that order—she went into her airy kitchen. Bending to smell the fresh flowers she kept on her small table for two, Esther took three seconds from her routine to take a deep breath and face another week. Marshall had texted her business number last night to confirm he needed a ride this Sunday morning, and that meant a long work week.

With the storm, though, Esther had already canceled all the jobs for Tuesday and until noon on Wednesday. Even the afternoon clients knew that it might not be safe to drive around the island after the storm. It was just too unpredictable, though Esther had never seen the weather shut down the island for very long.

Even if she wasn't driving that morning, she didn't make her own coffee. So she put her credit card and her driver's license—which she kept in a slim billfold—in her front right pocket, and a tube of mint Chapstick in her left. After shrugging into her jacket, she plucked the keys to the sleek, black Lincoln town car from the hook by the carport door and went outside.

The scent of sea and flowers met her nose, and she took another moment to savor it. She wasn't a Hawaii native, but she did enjoy living here.

She got behind the wheel and headed for The Roast down the street. Sunday didn't normally see too many people before six a.m., so there was no wait. Victoria leaned out of the window, her face brightening when Esther rolled down her window.

"Esther. Aloha. The usual?"

"Plus one," she said, which was her code to get her coffee as well as one for Marshall.

Vic knew how to make them, and she ducked back into the hut. Several minutes later, Esther lifted her to-go cup to her lips, the sweet caramel and the rich cream making the dark roast coffee delicious.

A sigh passed through her whole body and she twisted to accept the second cup.

Marshall's coffee. Regular roast. One splash of chocolate. One of milk. He took his richness in the cocoa, not the cream, and Esther had tried his concoction once, on a morning when he didn't need a ride. Vic hadn't been any the wiser, because Esther had gotten her usual too.

And while she thought nearly everything Marshall did was perfect, she much preferred her caramel cream concoction to his.

Not that it mattered. Marshall barely knew her name, and if he had to pick her out of line-up, Esther felt sure that he'd fail. Even the women he took to fancy dinners and business parties barely got a glance from him.

She handed over the cash for the coffees and eased the car back onto the road. It was a twenty minute drive up twisty, turny roads to Marshall's cliffside mansion. Esther could make the drive in her sleep, and sometimes she did. She never wore her power suits in those fantasies, but fun, flowy, flowery dresses, with flirty footwear and lip gloss the color of ripe raspberries.

Her hair flowed over her shoulders, and Marshall pushed it back to kiss her bare skin there.

She cleared her throat and her thoughts, and glanced at herself in the rear-view mirror. Maybe she seemed a bit flushed, but that could've been from the coffee, or the humidity. She completed the drive and parked with the front bumper right up at the gate.

Marshall never buzzed her in; she'd never seen the inside of his home. He came down the black, asphalt driveway, always wearing a perfectly tailored suit in black, gray, or navy blue. Esther much preferred the navy ones, and as he approached today, Esther didn't deviate from her routine.

She got five seconds to ogle him, and then she'd look straight through the windshield, acknowledge him professionally, and unlock the doors.

Today her five seconds saw him saunter toward her, so sexy and so untouchable it hurt. When her time was up, she turned and looked at her birthday gift for him on the back seat. Should she grab it now before he saw? What would he think?

She'd been driving him for years and never given him a birthday present. He'd never acted like it was his birthday on the day of, but he'd mentioned his summer birthdate a few years ago. Esther was a master at remembering small details. Her knack for it had kept customers loyal to her for long periods of time, and she trained all her drivers to pay attention to what people told them as they drove around the island.

She gave him a single nod and clicked the locks open. Marshall always sat on the passenger side, in the back seat. Today was no different. His long legs came first, followed by that toned body that must see hours in a gym.

Esther wrenched her thoughts from his body and watched as he spotted the blue-wrapped package on the seat.

"What's this?" He lifted it, the pale paper contrasting with his half-dark skin.

"Happy birthday, sir," Esther said.

He shook his head and started to chuckle. "You never cease to amaze me. How do you remember all that you do?"

"Oh, I can't reveal my secrets." She could also never reveal how warm his words made her.

"Should I open it?"

"Sure, go ahead."

He ripped the paper along the tape, always so proper. She wondered what it would be like to see him in a pair of shorts, casually eating with friends, or spending time with his family. She knew the Robison's were a tight-knit group, as she drove him to his parents' home every Thursday for dinner.

There really was so much to learn about a person just by watching them.

His laughter filled the car, and it was glorious. Esther wanted to bottle it and unstop it in the few moments before she fell asleep at night, so it could accompany her into sleep.

"A crossword puzzle book." He held it up for her to see, as if she didn't know what she'd wrapped. "Thank you, Esther." He gazed at the book with fondness, and when those dark eyes switched to her, he lit up her whole world.

She cleared her throat again and adjusted her sunglasses to make sure she wasn't giving anything away. That was another thing about Esther. She could hold an incredible amount of information and emotion close to the vest.

"Of course, sir," she said, flipping the car into reverse. She watched him covertly, and he flipped through the pages of the puzzle book, appreciation in his eyes. He glanced up at her a couple of times, but Esther kept both hands on the wheel and her eyes forward.

Marshall liked music, but nothing too loud. So the tropical tunes played at level three, and Esther's heart beat seemed to be bumping in time with them. Down, down, down she drove, and Marshall seemed to be watching her more than usual, which means he didn't immediately bury himself in his phone or something from his briefcase.

But he kept stroking his thumb along the cover of the puzzle book and looking at her. It was so out of his routine that by the time Esther pulled up to the pineapple plantation, she was positively jumpy. She managed to keep her hands still on the wheel though she felt like squirming and twitching.

Marshall also didn't heave a sigh and get out the way he normally did. He leaned forward like he might say something to her, but in the end, he settled back against the seat.

"Thank you again," he said, his voice like the hibiscus honey she loved in her evening tea. Warm, sweet, thick.

"Happy birthday," she said. "I hope the storm doesn't ruin it."

A smile lit up his face and he collected his coffee and his briefcase, and he got out of the car, the way he always did. He walked toward the steps, the same way he had yesterday and every day before that.

But then he paused, turned around, and looked at her. Seemingly right at her, despite the mirrored lenses and layers of glass between them.

Esther pulled in a breath and then pulled away from the curb, cursing herself for buying the man a birthday gift. She may as well have screamed, "I have a crush on you!" and left it at that.

# TWO

MARSHALL ROBISON STALLED at the top of the steps again, and he turned to watch the car he'd ridden in for years brake before pulling back onto the street. Something writhed inside him. Something he hadn't felt in a long, long time. Something he hadn't expected to feel again, frankly.

Attraction to a woman.

He shook his head and entered the building where all the official business for the Robison Plantations got done. He handled the majority of it, and he'd fallen behind on a few things last week as his grounds crew prepared for the storm coming in tomorrow night. Even a hefty wind could prove dangerous for his trees and his profits, so he took the storm warnings very seriously.

No one besides him would be in today, and honestly, that was how Marshall liked it. The southern plantation ran tours seven days a week, but he'd enjoy some relative peace up here at the largest and northernmost property.

As he settled into his office by opening the window and placing his coffee on the desk, he told himself that he wasn't attracted to Esther Pinnett. His *driver*, Esther. He'd been using her since his mother had given him a 30-day trial service for his thirtieth birthday. He'd always thought Esther a friend, though they didn't talk a whole lot. But he'd never really *looked* at her, at least not like he had this morning.

Of course, he never really looked at women at all. He took them to the required business functions, as required by his father.

His father….

"It's just your dad getting in your head," he muttered to himself, the memories from Thursday night's dinner streaming through his mind. So he was closer to forty than thirty. Closer to inheriting the entire plantation operation legally. Closer to his father's retirement. Closer to not having anyone to pass the plantations onto when he was ready to retire. At this point, he'd be seventy-seven before any of his offspring reached forty, the traditional age that the planta- tions were passed to their next inheritor in the Robison family.

So some things would have to change. That was all. That was what he'd told his father, and he'd come back with, "Well, that's if you get married and have a child in the next nine months."

Which Marshall was nowhere near doing.

"In fact," his dad had continued. "I haven't seen you out with the same woman twice in years."

*Not since Lorna.*

Even the name of his ex-wife erased any of that pesky attraction that *might* have been flowing through him in the town car.

Still, one of the first things he did after his laptop came to life was search Your Ride. Esther had a beautiful website, and he wondered if she built it herself or hired it out.

He clicked on the ABOUT tab and read that the company had been in business for fifteen years. A much younger version of Esther stood beside a black car, a wide, wonderful smile on her face as she held up a set of keys.

The whole story wasn't there, and Marshall wanted it. Maybe he wanted more to his life than a ride down the mountain to work, and dinner with his parents and sister on Thursday nights, and a few meetings with the other billionaires on the island from time to time.

And if he was going to start dating again, really dating, he wanted to start with Esther.

He pulled a folder toward him, wondering how to ask her out without coming across as too interested. Or not interested enough, like he just wanted to repay her for the crossword puzzles. Or as someone who wanted a second date with a woman when he hadn't done that in a long time.

Marshall sighed, unsure how to proceed. *Dating should be easier than this*, he thought as he opened the folder and focused on the financial report he'd neglected last week. The work distracted him for a few minutes, and then his phone buzzed.

Fisher.

Marshall's best friend since he'd come to the island

five years ago, looking to change the landscape of hospitality on the beach for good. Fisher had encountered a lot of resistance, mostly from smaller hotel and motel owners, but his tower on the beach was wildly popular and had brought a lot more people to Getaway Bay.

Marshall had wanted a piece of that tourism, and he'd partnered with Fisher early to have information about his pineapple plantations in every one of Sweet Breeze's four hundred and fifty-two rooms. His tour income had doubled in the ten months Sweet Breeze had been open, and Fisher and Marshall led the Hawaii Nine-0 club, which they'd founded for the island's billionaires about eighteen months ago.

Fisher probably wanted another meeting, and his attention wandered from the now-black phone and back to the numbers he needed to check against a report from his accountant. But the figures only kept his focus for about ten seconds, his mind pingponging back to his phone. Then Esther. Then his phone again.

"Text her," he muttered to himself. He had the woman's number. Sure, it was her work line, but she'd see the message and respond. She had a one-hundred percent response rate, after all.

He swiped the device from his desktop and unlocked it. Fisher had said *What are you doing for lunch today?* and Marshall normally would've told him to send a car and he'd join him in his twenty-eighth floor penthouse for the best seafood on the island.

Marshall loved seafood, and his mouth watered as all

he'd consumed that day was the delicious coffee that Esther brought him that morning.

How had he never *seen* her before now?

*Can't*, he thumbed out to Marshall. *Have something else going on.*

And that something else was going to be lunch with Esther. As soon as he gathered up his courage and stuffed away his fear and anxiety about starting a new relationship, then he'd text her.

His phone felt like a brick in his hand, and he still didn't message her. "She's not Lorna," he finally told himself and got his fingers in gear.

---

Noon found him walking through the smooth-gliding doors at Sweet Breeze. He felt like a hurricane, with emotions swirling and blowing inside him. Everyone around him obviously felt the low pressure system, because they gave him a wide berth as he navigated toward Fisher's private elevator and punched in the code to get the doors to open.

A slick, forty-three second ride later, and he entered Fisher's apartment. "Fish," he called, wiping his fingers across a shiny end table that had zero dust. Fisher's housekeeping department outperformed everyone, and it was no wonder he'd become a self-made billionaire in only a few years.

"What happened to your other plans?" Fisher appeared in the kitchen doorway, his sandy blond hair quite short. Marshall hadn't realized he'd gone so close to the scalp with the clippers, and a twinge of guilt flowed through him.

"They fell through." Marshall practically growled the words, not wanting to talk about how Esther had turned him down. *Turned him down.*

He'd never been so humiliated in his life. And he'd been forced to take a cab from the plantation to Sweet Breeze, and he was seriously considering doing it again this afternoon instead of redirecting Esther here so he could get home.

"Why are you grumpy?" Fisher indicated the bags on the dining table and added, "Those fried shrimp you like. Miso soup. Lobster sashimi."

Everything Marshall liked, and he sat down and opened the bag closest to him, hoping for the lobster first. But he found the soup and decided that was just fine. It came with a giant shrimp anyway, and Marshall started eating so he wouldn't have to answer Fisher's question.

He didn't want to tell Fish about Esther. Fisher hadn't dated anyone that Marshall knew of, and while they hadn't had a heart-to-heart about why neither of them had women in their lives, Marshall knew how much money complicated things. Fisher also didn't have to put on appearances if he didn't want to, a luxury Marshall didn't have.

"Okay, so I have a confession," Fisher said, sitting opposite of Marshall and opening another bag. He pulled out a couple of sushi rolls, which made Marshall frown. Didn't he know there was much better fish to be eaten?

"I didn't ask you to lunch because I like you." Fisher gave Marshall a grin. "I was hoping you'd let me tour one of your closed plantations."

Hardly anything surprised Marshall anymore. While his

curiosity soared over why Fish wanted a private tour, he didn't need all the details. "Sure. You name the time."

"I'm not sure yet, but I'll keep you updated." Fisher dug into the disgusting sushi rolls, and Marshall kept on with the soup. Could he ask Fisher about Esther? What would he even say?

He dismissed the idea and let the conversation take its normal track, which meant they talked about business, and profit margins, and Marshall's parents. Fisher came to dinner on Thursday nights sometimes, and for a while there, Marshall thought his little sister Marin would snag Fisher's attention.

But she hadn't, and Marin was dating a nice Hawaiian man now. Marshall desperately needed to follow her lead, so as soon as he finished eating, he moved to Fisher's couch and pulled out his phone.

*I'm at Sweet Breeze,* he typed out to Esther. *When would be the earliest you could come get me?*

He leaned back into the cushions, half-hoping she couldn't come until evening. Or that she wouldn't answer for a while, the way she hadn't when he'd asked her to lunch.

But his phone buzzed and her words said *Anytime, Mr. Robison. You tell me.*

He sighed, which drew Fisher's attention, and Marshall decided it was time to go. He could waste the afternoon in his huge house doing...something. So he heaved himself off the couch and said, "Thanks for lunch. See you on the other side of the storm."

Fisher looked alarmed, as if he didn't even know there

was a storm coming—and he probably didn't. Fish trusted too much to his general manager, and though Owen was a straight-laced guy and Marshall didn't think he'd ever lead Fisher astray, Marshall still would never put that much trust in another person.

He had before, and it had nearly ruined him.

He chuckled at Fisher's surprised look, pushed aside the thoughts of his ex-wife as he approached the elevator, and messaged Esther with *Is now okay? I'll wait outside.*

*I'll be there in ten minutes, sir.*

He hated the *mister* and the *sir.* Hated them like he never had before. In fact, Marshall usually liked the professionalism and respect he commanded from others. But all of a sudden, he didn't want the formal distance between him and her.

He went outside, the humidity and heat a pleasant reminder of where he lived. Fisher disliked the way the air felt like water in his lungs, but Marshall liked it. He'd grown up here, and there was nowhere he'd rather be.

The valet glanced at him, his eyebrows raised, and Marshall said, "Just waiting for my ride."

Sweet Breeze had a wide bay for drop-offs and pick-ups, and there always seemed to be a constant stream of rental cars, cabs, buses, and shiny town cars like the one Marshall was used to riding in.

At one-thirty, though, a couple of hours after check-out and a couple before check-in, the drive was mostly empty. Pacing from the lobby doors to the pillars that bordered a flower garden, Marshall tried to figure out what to say to Esther when she arrived.

Could she just not go to lunch that day? Maybe she'd been driving another client. She obviously cared about him.

"As a client, you dolt," he muttered to himself, stepping off the curb to head back to the lobby side. He hadn't taken one step before a horrible screeching sound ripped through his awareness, echoing around the chamber created by the hotel above and the road beneath.

He looked right just in time to see a black car bearing down on him, the driver wearing a panicked look on her beautiful face.

*Esther's here* passed through his mind as the car hit him and he tumbled to the ground.

# THREE

ESTHER'S CHEST heaved as the car came to a stop. A moan filled the space around her as she realized she'd just hit Marshall.

"Marshall!" She jumped from the car, all gears firing now. Anger and frustration and desperation mixed inside her, a dangerous cocktail that felt one second away from exploding. Today had been completely out of the ordinary, and she didn't know how to handle it.

But she could call an ambulance and make sure Marshall wasn't dead. With her phone at her ear, she knelt next to the man who'd been starring in her dreams for way too long. Marshall lay on the ground in his expensive suit, his dark hair a splash of light against the black asphalt. His eyes were closed, and he looked beautiful and at peace.

"Sir?" she asked as the valet came running over. "I didn't see him," she said to Sterling.

"He wasn't watching," Sterling said. "9-1-1?"

Esther nodded and pushed her sunglasses up onto her head as the operator answered. "I hit a man, and he's—" She stalled as Marshall opened his eyes and started laughing.

Esther wasn't sure if her heart was pounding because he was okay, or because he'd played a trick on her, or what. "I think he's okay."

"Are you sure?" the woman asked.

Marshall sat up, and he was clearly fine. Or at least fine enough not to warrant an ambulance.

"Yes," Esther said. "Sorry to bother you." She hung up and sat back on her haunches, the hard edges of her high heels digging into her skin. "Are you okay, sir?" She put her hand tentatively on his shoulder.

He sobered and looked at her hand, somehow making the moment between them charged and heated in that simple second.

Esther pulled her hand back, the words of his text flowing through her mind. *Want to go to lunch with me today?*

She had been completely flabbergasted by the text. Never, not once, had he ever asked her to have a meal with him. Most of the time, he barely looked at her, choosing instead to use the driving time to study his phone, or something from his briefcase, or stare blankly out the window as the tropical landscape passed and gave way to the rockier lava cliffs where he lived.

But lunch?

Why in the world would he invite her to lunch? He gave her his schedule on a weekly basis, and there was nothing on this slow Sunday to indicate he needed some arm candy at a business function.

Esther had a rolodex of excuses. She'd used almost all of them with some measure of success, throwing away the ones that didn't work and keeping the ones that did. She hadn't been out with a man in a while now, not willing to be told one more time that she was just a fling or already married to Your Ride.

Most men who wanted to go out with Esther weren't interested in the long-term, and she'd finally come to the conclusion that it was better not to date at all than to go out with a man once or twice and have him discard her for that week's newest flavor.

As she stared at Marshall, she realized she could totally be his newest flavor.

And she wanted long-term, and while Marshall was a native of the island and certainly not going anywhere, she hadn't been able to accept his lunch invitation. She'd had a job to do, and it involved driving three Japanese businessmen to the airport right during lunchtime.

She hadn't told him that, though. Just said, *I can't, sorry,* and moved on with her life. Because Marshall wasn't really interested in her. He probably just wanted to repay her for the crossword puzzle book. Or use her to appease his father. Neither of those were enticing reasons to go out with him, even if dinner with him was exactly what she'd dreamed about for months. Besides, he'd asked her to *lunch*, not dinner.

She glanced up, surprised when she found Marshall on his feet, dusting himself off. Sterling had obviously helped him stand, and Esther hurried to join them.

"I'm so sorry," she said. "There was this guy right on my

tail, and I turned in a little faster than I normally would have…." Her voice trailed off, hoping Marshall wouldn't fire her. Or say anything about her reckless driving. In a business where she literally had to have the cleanest driving record around, she couldn't afford to have any rumors about her hitting a client out there.

"I didn't see you," she finished lamely, glancing at Sterling. He'd back her up; he'd said Marshall wasn't even looking.

"It's fine." He brushed one last invisible bit of dirt from his jacket. "I'm fine." His eyes settled on hers, and the whole world fell away. He was looking right at her, something Esther hadn't experienced before.

His eyes, dark as night, consumed her, and she had no defense against him. He nodded to Sterling, who went back to his post at the valet station, and Marshall stepped toward the passenger side of the car.

"Sorry to demand sudden service," he said, opening the door but not sliding into the car.

"It's fine," she said, her voice a bit hollow. "I'd just finished another job."

He tilted his head at her, and it seemed like leagues separated them, not just the length of the town car. "Is that why you couldn't go to lunch with me?"

She nodded, her neck a little too tight. She moved to her door, which was still open, surprised into stillness when Marshall moved around the back of the car as if to intercept her.

"So maybe you could go to dinner." He spoke in a voice she'd never heard before, and she'd listened to him talk on the phone to his mom, his sister, his office manager, and other employees. He's never spoken in this soft, warm, honey-like voice.

All of her excuses fled, and she couldn't remember a single one. She didn't *want* an excuse for why she couldn't go out with him.

"Why?" she asked. As soon as the word left her mouth, she wanted to suck it back in.

"Why what?"

Fully committed, and honestly needing to know, she cocked her hip and folded her arms. "Why are you asking me out now?"

Something heated entered his eyes, a flirtatious glint maybe. Esther wasn't entirely sure, as she'd never seen Marshall like this before.

Marshall's jaw tightened for only a moment, but long enough for Esther to see it. "I'd like to get to know you better," he finally said.

The words were like a hallelujah chorus singing from heaven, and Esther had no idea what to do with them. "Does this have anything to do with your birthday gift?" She lifted her chin, almost daring him to say yes. "Or a business dinner you need a date for?"

"Of course not." He took another step toward her, almost within arm's reach now. "Just dinner with the two of us. A private dinner. I'll ask you questions about your life. I'll tell you things about mine." He shrugged like he went to a dinner as he described with a different woman every night, but Esther knew for a fact that he did not. He didn't own a car, and she drove him everywhere. The women he did go out with were one-night stands. One meal. A few hours, and then Esther nor Marshall ever saw them again.

*He could take a cab,* her mind whispered, but Esther was well-connected on the island, and she would've heard if one of the best looking, richest bachelors in Getaway Bay had been dating.

With a jolt, she realized that if she went out with him, she'd be the center of the gossip circles for a while. Stacey had started something with Fisher DuPont very recently, and there were already twitters about that.

"So?" he asked. "What do you think about dinner?" He wore a look of nervousness in his expression that endeared him to her.

"All right," she said, the carefully practiced reasons she'd used in the past nowhere to be found in her memory. "When?"

"When works for you?"

She wanted to blurt, "Tonight!" but she didn't want to come across more desperate than she already was. "I'm pretty busy preparing for the storm. Maybe Thursday?"

Marshall glanced away, telling Esther that Thursday was not a good day for him. But he said, "Sure, Thursday is fine."

A measure of relaxation sighed through her and a smile slipped across her face. "I'll come pick you up?"

His eyes came back to hers, and their powerful gaze seemed to increase her internal temperature by ten degrees. A smile twitched against his strong mouth, a gesture she rarely saw on Marshall's face. "Yeah, you better come pick me up. Is six too early?"

She shook her head, wondering how she was going to wait four whole days to see him again.

Which was silly, really. She'd see him tomorrow morning, same as always.

She nodded. "All right, then. Should we go?"

"Yeah, let's go." Marshall didn't move back to his side of the car, though. He put his hand on the driver's door and waited for Esther to slide into the car. Then he shut the door, walked around the hood and joined her in the front passenger seat.

Everything the man did made her nerves tingle, and Esther settled her sunglasses into place so she could maintain some measure of dignity for the drive up to the cliffs.

———

Esther dropped Marshall at his office the next morning, nothing strained between them. He'd changed the routine and sat up front with her again, but he didn't reach across the console and coffee cups to hold her hand. So maybe she'd fantasized that he would. Maybe she'd lain awake in bed last night for twenty minutes thinking about exactly that.

Instead, he'd talked about the storm and that he was going to Sweet Breeze to weather it and that he'd be ready at the plantation by four so she could get him to the hotel and get herself somewhere safe.

"All right?" he'd asked, one foot out of the car and one in. "You have somewhere safe to stay?"

"Four is fine," she said. "You'll be my last drop-off. And I'm staying at Sweet Breeze too."

He'd gotten out of the car then, adding a new item to their routine yet again when he reached the top of the steps and turned back to wave good-bye to her.

As she pulled into the wing house, she had absolutely no idea what she was doing. Dating Marshall Robison? And not even dating, at least not for four more days.

*Three and a half,* she told herself as she parked in front of George's wing house. She'd texted him last night after she and Stacey had exchanged a flurry of messages and agreed to meet for fried food and conversation before George opened for the day.

The front door was unlocked, and her brother stood behind the bar, bent over a notebook. "Morning, George." She gave her brother a big smile. "Thanks for doing this."

"The French fry platter?" He nodded toward the pastry box she carried. "Or will those be enough carbs?"

"Yes, French fries." Esther opened the box and took out the only mango guava muffin. "And I got this for you."

He took the muffin with a smile and headed for the kitchen door. "French fries, comin' right up."

Esther helped herself to the soda machine, filling two cups with her and Stacey's favorite cola. Then she moved to the corner booth where they always met and talked, setting down the drinks and the muffins before sliding onto the bench seat.

She exhaled, knowing Stacey had more to say this morning than Esther did. In fact, Esther was thinking of keeping Marshall her little secret for just a while longer.

Maybe until after the first date, which could honestly be a disaster.

Nerves paraded through her like ants as she thought about complicating her relationship with Marshall. He was one of her best clients, and what if their relationship caused her to lose him both personally and professionally?

She shook her head and reached for her drink. A moment later George came back into the bar from the kitchen and resumed his spot in front of the notebook. Esther considered eating a muffin to quell her anxiety, but Stacey pushed into the wing house before she could.

The gorgeous redhead exchanged a glance with George and headed toward to the corner booth. Esther couldn't help feeling safe with her best friend. They'd been through a lot together over the years, and Esther trusted her explicitly. It had been Stacey who'd encouraged Esther to start Your Ride. Stacey who'd been her first customer. Stacey who'd been by her side through her break-ups. And vice versa. Esther had been there for Stacey when her fiancé skipped town and then after she'd found out her second fiancé had another girlfriend on another island.

They'd started the Women's Beach Club together, and it had been an incredible support group for both of them, as well as several other women on the island.

"Hey." Stacey slid into the booth and selected a blueberry muffin covered in large sugar crystals.

"Morning, sunshine." Esther gave her a lopsided smile, relaxing even further.

Stacey fiddled with the paper on the muffin, something clearly bothering her. Esther wouldn't pry. Stacey would talk when she was ready. That was how they worked. If they had something to gripe about or something to take to the whole group, they met on the beach. If it was something just between the two of them, they came to the wing house.

Esther scraped her thin hair into a ponytail while Stacy pinched off a piece covered with sugar and popped it into her mouth. Esther was just about to blurt out everything about Marshall when she saw George exit the kitchen with her food. She held the tidal wave of words back, desperate for the grease before she spilled her guts.

"You girls okay here?" He smiled down on them as he set a huge basket of French fries on the table. A platter of dipping sauces came next, and he settled his weight on his back leg.

"Just fine," Esther said, flashing her older brother a smile.

He took the cue and left. Stacey swirled a fry through the spicy ranch sauce and ate it, and Esther decided she could play this game too. She pick up several fries and dragged them through her brother's famous garlic aioli before taking a big bite.

"I kissed Fisher DuPont," Stacey blurted, almost causing Esther to choke. She held back the action, because she and Stacey had promised to always accept the other's decisions. Talk. Give advice. But accept.

"And look, it's not that big of a deal," Stacey continued. "Because it's not like he'll stay interested for long, and I'm sure this is just a summer fling."

Esther chewed, swallowed, and stared at her, her own confession slowly building beneath her tongue. "There's no law that says you can't date him."

"Well, there kind of is," Stacey said. "At least with you and the other women in the Beach Club."

"It's unspoken, not written."

"So what? I'll have to leave? I won't be invited to meetings anymore?"

Esther shrugged like it was no big deal. "I'm sure some of them will understand."

"Tawny," Stacey said.

Esther loved Tawny, but she couldn't argue with Stacey. Out of all the women in the Beach Club, Tawny had definitely been the most reluctant to join. She still believed in all the good things about love, and she wanted to find the man of her dreams.

Esther hadn't had the heart to tell her that no such man existed. Instead, she picked up another handful of French fries and coated them in the siracha ketchup.

Stacey narrowed her eyes at her. "What's going on with you?"

"Nothing." But the two syllables said anything but nothing.

"Esther," Stacey warned. "You better spill it right now. I told you about Fisher."

Esther sighed and sucked on her straw, draining half the cola in her cup while she tried to get the words to line up. "All right. There's something."

Stacey put her arms on the table, waiting. Esther looked at her, almost wishing she could just relay the information through a mind meld or something.

"I got asked out on a date," she said.

Surprise lifted Stacey's eyebrows, and her eyes started to

sparkle. "Oh. That's not bad. I was expecting you to say you'd been sued or something."

"No, no," Esther said, waving her hand over the French fries. "Your Ride is fine."

"So. A date." Stacey smiled. "Who was it? How did you let him down gently?"

Esther squirmed in her seat, unable to confess that all her excuses had dried up at the gorgeous sight of Marshall only a few feet from her, looking at her like he was truly interested.

"Well? Who was it?" Stacey asked.

"Marshall Robison." Esther eyed the French fries and pushed them away, her grease quota met for the day.

"The pineapple plantation Marshall Robison? The man you've driven around the island for two years? The one you have a crush on?"

Well, she didn't have to speak with quite so much disbelief in her tone. Esther nodded, a measure of sparkle shooting through her now too. "And I didn't let him down gently. I said yes."

Stacey stared for three long moments and then burst into laughter.

Happiness pulled through Esther, and she joined Stacey, only sobering long enough to tell her best friend, "You know he and Fisher are good friends, right? We should double," because the thought of going out with Marshall alone had every nerve in Esther's body firing like crazy.

# FOUR

MARSHALL GLANCED around his spacious house, his bag already packed. He'd done it that morning but had forgotten to grab it when he'd seen Esther pull up to his gate. He realized that he'd kept a huge, black lava rock wall around his life and heart for far too long.

Heck, he never even let Esther come all the way onto his property to pick him up. Today, he'd told her the code to his gate, and she'd driven him right up to the front door. Well, as close as she could get with the half-dozen steps leading to his double-wide front doors.

He'd said, "I'll be right back," instead of inviting her into the house. That felt too intimate, and they hadn't even gone out yet. None of the women he'd been out with had been to his house, and it was like a fortress only he was allowed inside.

The rides up and down the mountain hadn't been awkward, and Marshall found he was quite good at small talk. Esther didn't seem terribly relaxed around him, and as he lifted his bag, he knew why.

He'd been formal and stiff with her for seven years. She was acting exactly how he'd trained her to act.

*Not anymore*, he told himself as he moved behind the free-standing stairs to collect his bag. He couldn't stand on the patio, thinking about it any longer. He'd hired men to board all his windows and tie down anything outside worth keeping. The money he'd left on the kitchen counter that morning was gone, and his house was as ready for the storm as it could be.

The beach below had frothed with waves, and he was jeopardizing his own safety—and Esther's—by taking too long to muse over his closed-off life.

A deep internal groan started in his stomach when he remembered all the times Esther had driven him and a date somewhere. He had a lot of business functions, and to appease his father, he always brought a date.

A different woman every time, but still. A date.

What did Esther think about that? She'd probably driven him on two dozen first dates, her hands always at ten and two on the steering wheel, her eyes straight forward. A pure professional.

He grabbed the bag and hurried back to the car, his thoughts tumbling through his mind the same way the waves beat against the shore.

Esther stood beside the passenger door, her hair whipping in the wind and her arms folded to keep her jacket tight against her body. She was glorious and beautiful, and the attraction that had zipped through Marshall the previous day hit him like lightning. He felt like he was being tossed in the waves of the tropical storm about to hit the island, and when she turned her ocean-blue eyes on him, she positively stole his breath.

"Got it," he said, wondering what it would be like to go on a second date with her. Fantastic, most likely.

She reached for the door handle at the same time he did. His hand covered hers, causing fireworks to shoot through his bloodstream. "I've got it," he said, gazing down at her. "You don't have to open my door."

"You're paying me to drive you," she said. "I always open your door."

"Not anymore," he said. "You're off the clock." He inched forward, nearly pressing her against the car. She lifted her free hand to push her hair out of her face, and when she tilted her head back to keep her eyes on his, she exposed a beautiful length of neck that made Marshall's heart beat faster. "All right? I can open my own door."

"So I won't get paid to drive you to Sweet Breeze?" An edge entered her eyes that he couldn't tell was flirtatious or challenging.

"Of course you will. But I still want to open my own door. You didn't need to get out in the storm."

She softened and let her hand drift to his shoulder. She rested it there, electricity popping between them, before sliding her chilly fingers along his neck and finally touching his ear.

He shivered, and not only from the way the wind had reduced the temperature.

"I like you." The wind stole her voice almost before it entered his ears, making it soft, a whisper, there then gone.

She moved laterally, gently tugging her hand from beneath his, and stepped around the hood of the car. He opened his door in sync with her, and they got in the car together. He set his bag at his feet and pulled the door closed to keep the wind at bay.

"Sorry I made us late," he said.

"We'll be fine. Fisher isn't closing the doors until seven o'clock."

"We're forty minutes away," he said. "At least."

Esther pinned him with a look that was definitely flirty this time. "Plenty of time to talk then." She put the car in drive and eased around his circle drive. "You can start with your family. Siblings?"

"A sister, Marin. My parents. My father's family came to the island generations ago, to grow pineapples. My mom is a native Hawaiian."

She glanced at him, turning her attention quickly back to the twisty roads. "That's why you're so tall."

"Why?"

"You have mixed blood."

He half-shrugged. "Yep. What about you?"

"My family moved here when I was fourteen," she said, keeping her eyes on the road. Her usual mirrored sunglasses were gone, as the sky was the color of well water, with angry gray clouds obscuring most of the light. "My dad can work from home, and we needed a fresh start."

"Oh yeah? Why's that?"

Her fingers flexed on the wheel, and Marshall regretted asking. "You don't—"

"My oldest brother was killed in a car accident." She flicked her eyes at him again. "We moved here from Florida, because, well, none of us were dealing with Sean's death very well."

A pin of regret pushed into Marshall's heart. "I'm so sorry." He reached over and gently eased one of her hands off the wheel, stroking the back of it with his thumb. "Sorry I —I shouldn't have asked."

"It's okay." She squeezed his fingers. "It was a long time ago, but sometimes memories come quick and they hurt for a minute." She put a smile on her face, and though it wasn't one of her happy ones, it still made her radiant and strong. "We go back to Florida every year, usually in the winter. Hawaii's been good for my family."

"Good," Marshal repeated, glad he hadn't caused too much pain for her with his tactless questions. "You seem close to your family, then?"

"Yeah, close enough. I mean, we don't have a family dinner every week." She sucked in her breath and looked at him fully now, understanding in those gorgeous eyes. "We can't go out on Thursday. You have your family dinner."

He waved his free hand like the family dinner was nothing. "It's fine. I already got out of it. It's not like I go every week."

"You do, too," she said. "I drive you, Marshall. I *know*." Her grin this time was much flirtier than the sad one belonging to her brother.

He chuckled, wondering if he'd ever be able to do something to surprise Esther. Not likely when he didn't have his own car and relied on her to get him everywhere. She may not know what he did at Sweet Breeze, the plantation, or the numerous other places she drove him, but she knew his schedule. Knew who he'd been out with....

"Thursday's fine," he said, tightening his grip on her hand. "I don't want to wait another night to go to dinner with you."

"You know," she said. "We could eat together tonight. We'll both be at Sweet Breeze, and I got an email from their concierge about all the food they're offering for the shelterees."

Marshall made a face before he could stop himself. "I mean, if you want."

"Oh, is the food at Sweet Breeze beneath your standards?" Esther giggled, the sound free and fun, another couple of things that Marshall didn't allow into his life.

"Maybe."

"Oh, the challenge is on," she said, ramping up into laughter now. "We'll get settled, and then I'll take you around to all the restaurants and vendors until I find something worthy of the great Marshall Robison."

"I'm not that great," he muttered, though he enjoyed her laughter and the thought of spending a couple of hours with her tonight appealed to him greatly. And hey, if this counted as a date, Thursday night would make number two, and that was more dates than Marshall had had with the same woman in seven years.

"So what do you like?" she asked.

"Don't tell me you don't know." He chuckled and

twisted toward her, enjoying this conversation more than he had any other female chat.

"How would I know?" Her voice was a little strained and a little too high.

"You drive me everywhere," he said. "And I don't know how to cook."

"So seafood," she said. "I'm not sure what Sweet Breeze has to offer in the way of seafood."

"They have a sushi bar on the third floor," Marshall said. "It's trash."

Esther's laughter filled the car again, and Marshall couldn't help his instantaneous smile. "What?" he asked.

"It's true. *Sushi* should not be said in the same sentence as *bar*."

"You're a sushi snob."

"No." He'd deny that until the day he died. "I don't like sushi at all."

"No? A Hawaii native who doesn't like sushi?"

"I like sashimi," he said. "Big difference."

"Ooh," she said, her tone so full of flirt that Marshall's heart skipped a beat. He'd been flirted with plenty of times. He knew what it looked like, sounded like, felt like.

But it had never felt like this before, because he'd never wanted to reciprocate. He'd never even wanted to be on the receiving end of a woman's flirtations, at least not since his divorce.

"I like burgers too," he said to cover up how he felt inside. "And Fisher has a place called The Breezeway that serves a decent Hawaiian one, with barbeque sauce and grilled pineapple."

"Pineapple from the Robison empire?" Esther asked.

"Of course," Marshall said matter-of-factly. "Have you had my pineapple?"

Esther gave him a flirty grin and simply filled the car with laughter again. Marshall wasn't sure what was so funny, but it didn't really matter. It sure felt good to be riding beside her instead of behind her, the shape of her hand in his an exact fit.

———

The lobby was nearly deserted when he and Esther stepped through the doors. Fisher had told him to go up to the fourth floor, where Owen would have his room key, so they got on the elevator with several other people and went up.

A makeshift front desk had been set up, and dozens of employees were trying to get the hoard of people checked in and to their rooms. With the storm only hours from landfall, Marshall was glad he'd arranged his room early.

Owen worked behind the row of check-in clerks, and Marshall went down to the end of the tables and flagged him down.

"Oh, Marshall." Owen took something out of his inside breast pocket and handed it to him. "Your key. You're on the third floor."

Marshall leaned on the table with both hands. "Can you help me with Esther Pinnett?" he asked in a quiet voice. He didn't need the other guests getting worked up that he'd cut in line.

Owen's doesn't-miss-anything gaze gravitated over

Marshall's shoulder, where he could somehow feel Esther hovering.

"It's fine," she said. "I'll just get in line. It's moving fast." Marshall held up his hand to get her to wait, and he looked at Owen again. "Real quick." He flashed one of his best smiles, the kind that kept money in his bank account and everyone feeling like they'd gotten what they wanted.

"Give me a moment." Owen stepped out from behind the table and went into the theater, which was vibrating with bodies and energy.

Marshall returned to Esther's side, who once again tried to get in line. "He's doing it now," he said. "Give him a minute."

"Are you used to getting special favors?" She gazed up at him, and he had the craziest urge to tuck her hair behind her ear. He literally hadn't looked at another woman like this in the longest time.

"Yes," he said simply.

Owen returned a moment later—hardly a minute had passed—and handed Esther a small envelope. "You're on the seventh floor, Miss Pinnett."

"Thank you, Owen," she said. "And thanks for getting those new contracts signed so quickly."

"Well, you're the best." Owen flashed her a tight smile and moved behind the desk again.

Marshall watched the exchange, not quite sure what to make of it.

"I'm going to go get settled," Esther said. "Get out of these heels. Should we meet down here in say, a half an hour?"

Marshall tore his eyes from Owen and said, "Sure. Half an hour."

Esther accompanied him to the elevator, but as they were going different directions, he said good-bye to her when the car came that was going up. He stood in the hub-bub, hoping he wasn't making the biggest mistake in the world by starting a real relationship with someone.

Not just someone.

Esther, the woman he had to see every day of his life. If things went south, she would be very hard to cut out of his day-to-day existence.

*Then don't mess up with her*, he told himself as an elevator going down arrived. *Don't mess this up.*

# FIVE

ESTHER HURRIED to her room on the seventh floor, but she didn't get herself settled. She made phone calls to each of her employees to make sure they'd dropped off their last client for the day and were getting somewhere safe.

Three of them—Henry, Zaylia, and Eamon—were night drivers and hadn't started their shift due to the storm. They checked in quickly, and she marked them off her list. Henry and Zaylia were here at Sweet Breeze, and Esther was glad for that, as Henry lived in a house that was more of a hut right on the beach.

Jaylani Kawai was a single mom who didn't need to work. Her husband had died last year, and he'd had loads of life insurance. But Jaylani knew everyone on the island, and she liked the interaction with the people she drove, so she worked while her kids were in school, and she was one of Esther's best drivers.

She didn't check in, and Roger, Regina, and then Fern all confirmed that their clients had been delivered safely and they were either safe or on their way to somewhere safe. Esther kicked off her heels and paced the hotel room, waiting for Jaylani to text.

"Come on, Jay," she whispered to herself as the minutes ticked by. It was barely six o'clock, which meant Jaylani had plenty of time to get home or somewhere safe. But she wasn't one to ignore texts.

Her phone buzzed, and Esther checked it immediately, her heart bobbing in the back of her throat. When Marshall's name flashed on the screen, her pulse thumped harder.

*I'm down at The Breezeway. They close at eight-thirty, so plenty of time.*

*Waiting on an employee to check in,* she texted him. Although, she figured she could wait downstairs at The Breezeway as easily as she could in her room.

*Take your time,* he sent back at the same time she thumbed *On my way.*

She smiled, completely unsure of what she was doing, but her feet taking her out of the room and down the hall to the elevator nonetheless. Maybe this could be a real relationship. Maybe it could be a good thing.

But Esther wondered how much of that was true, and how much was just her wishful thinking, her absurd fantasies. She wished she could call an emergency session of the Beach Club, but with the weather, it would be at least the weekend before she could talk to her girlfriends and figure out what to do.

By then, she could have completed her second date with Marshall. She exited the elevator on the nearly deserted first floor with the words, *Marshall doesn't go on second dates,* running through her mind.

But as he pushed away from the marble pillar, wearing a more casual pair of jeans that still looked like they cost a thousand dollars and a black polo that made his muscles positively bulge. She really hoped he'd consider a second date with her.

He grinned at her as she came closer, and she felt sure she was hallucinating. In what reality was this her life? If someone would've told her even yesterday morning that she'd be going to dinner during a tropical storm with Marshall Robison, she'd have laughed in their face.

And now…he extended his hand for her to take, and she couldn't help the girlish giggle that tickled her throat. She told herself to stop doing that. She didn't want to be another of Marshall's giggly girlfriends. She wouldn't be.

"When do you find time to work out?" she asked him.

"I have a home gym," he said without missing a beat. "And insomnia."

"You don't sleep?" Esther had packed some lavender oil that would help with that. He should probably take ashwaganda in the morning and melatonin right before bed too. She bit back her homeopathic suggestions, though, deciding to keep that little quirk about herself a secret for now.

"I mean, I sleep," he said, lifting two fingers for the hostess.

"Is the bar okay?" she asked.

He shook his head and said, "A table or a booth. Not the bar." He reached into his pocket and pulled out a bill.

Esther couldn't catch the number on it before he slipped her the bill, and she smiled at him and said, "Right this way." She seated them in a tiny booth built for two, and Marshall didn't open the menu given to him.

"You already know what you want." Esther had never eaten here before, and in fact, she felt a bit uneasy being here at Sweet Breeze. Stacey had disliked the place so much, and Esther had supported her through her year-long worry-fest and fight against the monstrous hotel. But once the permits were in place, and the building started, Stacey had given up the fight.

She owned a five-room bed and breakfast just down the beach from Sweet Breeze, but Esther hadn't noticed her losing any money because of the new hotel. Stacey had stayed here on Thursday to gather some intel, and that had snowballed into a relationship with kissing in only a few days.

Did Esther dare to hope for the same?

She scanned the menu, not really reading the items. "What's good?" she asked.

"You want authentic or American?"

Esther set the menu down and leaned her elbows on it. "How about you order for me?"

Surprise lifted Marshall's eyebrows, followed immediately by an edge of desire in the dark depths of his eyes.

Her phone buzzed, and she pulled it from her pocket. She had only changed her shoes before coming downstairs, and she wished she'd been able to put on one of the flirty dresses she'd fantasized about. But she hadn't packed anything like that. She'd hopefully only be here for one night, and she'd been practical in what she'd put in her bag.

"Oh, thank the stars," she said with relief as she read that Jaylani had finished for the night and was headed home. "My last driver is done."

"Great." Marshall grinned at her. "So now you can relax."

She almost snorted. Did he know how wound up she always was in his presence? Well, not always. Just since he'd come out of his house with a gray cat she'd never seen before. When she'd questioned him about the tabby, he'd told her it didn't belong to him. That it belonged to a family down the road, plantation workers of his.

But though it wasn't his, he left food and water out for it, and Popoki—the cat's name—somehow found his way into Marshall's house from time to time.

"And that's okay with you?" Esther had asked, her eyes trained on him in the rear view mirror.

He'd shrugged. "I don't know. I kind of like it. Means I don't have to come home alone."

At that moment, Esther had felt something vulnerable in him she'd overlooked before. He seemed more human, and while he'd always been drop-dead gorgeous, suddenly he was touchable where he'd been so out of reach before.

Of course, he'd still been completely out of Esther's league, but her fantasies had started that day she'd seen him carry the not-his-cat out of the house and gently set him on the lawn.

The waitress came, and Marshall kept his eyes pinned on

Esther's as he ordered her a strawberry peach pineapple smoothie.

It was seriously the sexiest thing a man had ever done for her, and Esther had difficulty staying still. Her skin itched, her blood writhed in her veins, and her muscles twitched.

"Do you know what you want?" the girl asked, leaning one hip into the table and turning her back on Esther completely.

"Oh, I think I know exactly what I want."

Esther cleared her throat and ducked her head, suppressing a smile and a laugh.

"I'll take the angus sliders," he said. "And the bacon cheese fries, and…a BLTA, with sweet potato fries and mango pineapple relish." His eyes glittered like dark diamonds, and Esther seriously could've drowned in them.

The waitress walked away without writing anything down, and Esther asked, "What's a BLTA?"

"Bacon, lettuce, tomato, and avocado," he said. "Locally grown avocadoes, I might add."

She shook her head. "How did you know I have a weakness for both bacon and fruity drinks?"

He cocked his head and then shook it, his hair flopping a little with the motion. "Maybe you're not the only one who can be observant."

Esther scoffed. "I have never eaten bacon or drunk anything but coffee in front of you."

"Coffee with caramel," he said.

Disbelief tore through her. They didn't talk as they went from his house to work. Not really. A few things here and there. Superficial things. "How do you know that?"

"I can smell it every morning," he said.

"You should try it."

"I like my chocolate just fine." He glanced up as the drinks arrived. Esther's was massive, a glass at least ten inches tall and bulbous at the bottom and skinny at the top. He'd ordered nothing, but the waitress set down a water before she turned away.

Their food came quickly, and the conversation was light and easy. Marshall was quite a good conversationalist, and Esther liked the sound of his voice as he told her about the tree house he'd built one summer when he was fifteen, and how he'd worked on the family pineapple plantations starting at age five.

Dinner lasted barely an hour, and Marshall stepped onto the elevator with Esther's hand in his. He went up with her and when the car dinged at floor seven, he got off and walked with her down the hall.

Her heart beat faster with every step, and she paused when she was a few feet from her door. "Okay, so just tell me straight up. Was that our first and last date?"

Something akin to hurt passed over his face and he fell back a step. "No. We're set for Thursday." His voice broke on the last syllable, but it was strong when he added, "For date number two."

Esther could tell the words cost him something. But he was a billionaire, and she hoped he could afford them.

"Great." Esther tipped up on her toes and gave Marshall a quick peck on the cheek. "Stay safe during the storm." Then she ducked inside her room as quickly as possible, wanting to kiss Marshall properly but absolutely terrified of it at the same time.

She pressed her back into the locked door, both palms against the metal. She had plenty of money too, but what she hoped was that her fragile heart could handle it when Marshall decided he'd had enough dates with her. If not, she'd have pieces from the bay to the cliffside manor where she'd still have to drive every day.

# SIX

MARSHALL ARRIVED at the two-room suite he was sharing with Owen and his sons to find all three of them there. The two teens wore basketball shorts and T-shirts, their eyes riveted to the television. The younger of the sons —Zach—held a basketball in his hands, twisting and twirling it unconsciously.

Owen still wore his suit as he leaned forward to peer at something on his laptop. Then he clicked and started sending a text.

"Hey," he said while he did that. "How was dinner?"

Marshall collapsed in the armchair opposite them, the TV blaring right in his ear. "Great." And it really was the first meal he'd shared with a female not related to him that hadn't felt like torture.

Owen gave half a smile, all he seemed capable of as absorbed as he was in his work. "Fisher needs me for a few minutes." He stood and gathered various devices before heading for the door.

"You just got back from Fisher's," Cooper, his oldest son, said.

"Yeah, one more thing." Owen opened the door and left. Marshall watched the two teens, who certainly didn't need a babysitter in the hotel. It wasn't like they could go anywhere during the storm.

"What's this?" he asked, leaning forward to take a look at the TV.

"Corn hole," Zach said, still spinning that ball.

"On TV?" Marshall shook his head. "That's what people play in their backyards. How is this a sport?"

"It's not," Cooper said. "But he gets to watch it until nine-thirty, and then I get the remote."

"The storm's supposed to make landfall about then," Marshall said. "Do you think your dad will be back by then?"

"Yeah." Cooper reached for a candy bar on the table in front of him, and Marshall copied him. "I guess Fisher's girl-friend is coming for a late dinner."

"Ah." Marshall suspected that Owen would know all the details about that, but Marshall didn't really need to know. Fisher would tell him—or he wouldn't. It wasn't like they discussed their relationships in great detail.

He leaned back into the chair and closed his eyes, the ruckus on TV more annoying than he liked. "Well, I think I'll get some work done too." He opened his eyes and stood up. "Am I in the second bedroom?"

"Yeah," Cooper said. "Me and Zach are in the master, and Dad's taking the sofa bed out here."

"Thanks, guys." He unwrapped his chocolate as he went into the bedroom and closed the door. He'd already put his bag in the room when he'd come to change, and he closed the door and just let the silence soak in.

The wind beyond the glass indicated that the storm was closer, and Fisher pulled back the drapes to find only darkness. He didn't think it quite late enough to be so black, further testifying of the magnitude of the storm.

His phone went off, and he checked it, hoping it was Esther, maybe just saying good night. As if she hadn't already.

But it was Fish. *You went to dinner with a woman?*

Marshall frowned, his defenses flying right into place. His relationship with Esther wasn't any of Fish's business. So he tossed his phone onto the dresser and changed into his pajamas.

This time of night usually found him on the treadmill, but for once, he actually felt tired. So he put the TV on the Weather Channel and muted the volume.

When he woke, a hint of sunlight seeped through the crack in the curtains. He showered and put on one of his suits, knowing he'd need to make an appearance at all of the plantations that day. His foremen would be there, as instructed, if the weather was good, and as Marshall whipped back the drapes and looked outside, it seemed like the storm was completely gone.

Of course, that wasn't entirely true. Debris and downed branches were everywhere. But at least the storm surge seemed to have been overestimated. He wondered what his yard would look like. He wasn't worried about the ocean reaching his house, but the wind up in the cliffs could be murder on a normal day.

Owen handed him a cup of coffee when he went out into the main area, but it was too bitter and too hot to drink. Marshall said, "Thank you," anyway, and "Yes," when Owen asked him if he wanted to go see Fisher that morning.

"Your Ride contracts," Owen muttered. "Guest projections. Food costs." He tucked everything in his briefcase and said, "Ready."

Marshall watched him with a wary eye, wondering if Fisher had signed on to contract Your Ride exclusively.

The activity at the hotel seemed to be at an all-time high as Owen led the way to his office. "I don't think he'll be in there," Marshall said.

"We always meet in my office." Owen seemed a little cooler than usual, but Marshall supposed he was simply overworked, what with all the extra guests and moving everything up to higher levels.

Owen opened the door, and sure enough, Marshall stood at the fish tank, staring. "Oh, he is in here."

Marshall hated that Owen was right, especially when the man threw him a triumphant look before turning to Fish with surprise.

Fisher put his hands in his pockets. "We made it through the storm." Ever the calculating, thinking type, he looked a bit grim.

"Sure did." Owen settled behind his desk and disappeared behind his computer. *Some meeting*, Marshall thought.

Yet Fisher loved the guy, and Marshall was glad Owen did such a stellar job. And he liked Owen's kids too. Heck, Owen himself was just fine. He'd just been acting a bit weird the last couple of days.

"Can I talk to you?" Marshall asked Fish, wondering what the text last night had been about. "Have you been back up to your suite yet?"

"Not yet. Let's go get my bag and head up there."

"Can you get some of those spinach soufflés sent up?"

"Owen?" Fisher asked.

The general manager picked up the phone and pushed a button. Marshall didn't wait to hear what Owen said. He left, fully expecting the soufflés to be hot and waiting when they finally got to the twenty-eighth floor.

Marshall wasn't sure why he was so on-edge today, but he suspected it had a lot to do with Esther and how badly he wanted to see her again.

———

Fisher picked up a Rubix cube as soon as he entered his suite. Four completed puzzles sat on the dining room table, and Marshall watched his friend rotate the panels on the cube around and around at the speed of light.

He'd never been attracted to the cube. But puzzles intrigued him. Riddles. Anything that was clever, and witty, and a little twisted. He looked away from Fish and sat on the couch. "You signed new contracts with Your Ride?"

"Sounds familiar."

"Do you know the owner?"

"Esther Pinnett, sure. Does a lot of the driving herself."

"She does all of my driving," Marshall said. "And she's Stacey's best friend."

Fisher looked away from the colored squares on the cube. "I didn't know that."

"I'm going out with her on Thursday." Marshall swallowed back the words that it would be their second date.

Fisher abandoned the Rubix cube completely. "Esther? You?"

"Don't sound so shocked."

"What party do you have coming up?"

"This isn't for a party." Marshall drummed his fingers on the table, unsure why the uneasiness had chosen now to romp through him.

"I've never seen you pay any attention to women for anything but business."

"I could've said the same for you." Marshall looked at him out of the corner of his eye. "But now you've got Stacey staying with you until all hours of the night."

Fisher scoffed. "I do not."

"That's not what Owen said on the way up."

"Owen doesn't need to monitor me twenty-four-seven."

Marshall chuckled. "Well, he does."

"It was barely past midnight," he said. "And I was asleep for at least two hours before that."

"Sounds romantic." Marshall watched Fisher, wondering if he could really go out with Esther again. "You like her?" Fish asked.

"I do."

Marshall nodded, realizing that he liked Esther too. He

always had. But this new animal in his chest was different than what he'd felt for his driver before. That had been admiration for her professionalism. A general liking for her as a friend. But now he thought about holding her hand and kissing her, and that was a whole new level of like he hadn't experienced in a long time.

"We're not normal men, you know? There's so much to consider when getting involved with a woman." He exhaled, wishing his emotions could go as easily as his breath. "How did you know I had dinner with her last night?"

"Owen," Fish said, his focus on his phone. Marshall seethed the tiniest bit. Was Owen monitoring him too? And why? He was just a guest here, and Owen had no right to pay him more attention than he would anyone else.

But he laughed with Fisher and made a joke about his next date with Stacey. Then he got out of there, determined to see the damage the storm had done to his plantations and still have time to call Esther before the day slipped away from him.

---

Marshall tucked his pants into a pair of black, rubber boots before going out into the plantation with Alai. "Things must be bad," he commented.

Alai, a Hawaiian about a decade older than Marshall, looked like he'd rolled around in a mud pit and then stuck his head under a spigot to get clean. "It's not too bad, boss."

"Right." Marshall finished and followed his foreman at the northern plantation out the door. The rows and rows of green pineapple plants had always brought a measure of peace to Marshall's soul, and today was no different.

Sure, some of the taller leaves had been blown clean off. There were unripe clusters of flowers—what would become a pineapple—on the ground. Some swampy areas in already loamy and sandy ground where the rain had pooled and their drainage systems had overfilled. But overall, this section of the field had taken the storm well.

"The upper leaves took the brunt of the wind," Alai said. "But the wind blocking helped that new fifteen acres on the northwest side."

"So that was a good idea," Marshall said. And it had been his idea. Their fences were normally just chain link, which wind could blow through easily. They planted new plants around the edges of the fields and he'd been worried about them. So he'd done some research and found that some farmers in windy parts of the world put sheets of plastic around their chain link to block the wind. He'd put his crew on it as soon as the weather warning had come in.

"A great idea," Alai confirmed. He went through the clean up procedures, how they needed more bamboo for their drainage troughs, and how long he thought it would take the people they already employed.

"A week?" Marshall asked, bending to pick up what had once held a pineapple and had been ripped up—a sucker. Everything on the plantation was done by hand, except for the plowing and fertilizing. But the neat rows were done by hand. The harvesting was done by hand. The packaging and shipping was done by hand.

Marshall's plantations were the single biggest employer

of people on the island, even beating Fisher's twenty-eight story hotel by a couple dozen workers.

"I'll get both crews out here to go through the rows," Alai said. "They'll inspect the suckers and slips, as normal, and we'll get them all categorized. But I need people to prep the new fields for them, if we want to get them replanted right away."

And Marshall did. It took months to grow pineapples; it wasn't something done overnight. His family had the planting, the fertilizing, the ethylene application, all down to a science. Everything on each plantation happened like clockwork, so there was no wasted time, no wasted land, no wasted money or manpower.

Alai watched him, and Marshall ran his fingers along another cluster of flowers in the dried flower stage; this one had survived the wind and rain. "I'll get an extra crew in."

"Sounds good, boss."

Marshall walked down another row, chatting with Alai about their plants, their process, more clean up talk, and finally his family. Then he got behind the wheel of one of the trucks they used for local delivery and went to the next plantation.

Each had a foreman for him to meet with. Each required a new pair of boots to go out into the soft dirt of the fields. Each had some measure of devastation, loss, and rebuilding that needed to be done. Each could've fared worse.

When he got to the tourist plantation on the south side of the island, the damage there was much, much worse than the other three fields. The storm had swirled on this side of the island for longer and had actually made landfall here at some point during the night.

As it was the public face of Robison Plantations, Marshall said to the foreman, "How long do we need to shut down the tours?"

Yuji, a petite woman in stature but powerful when it came to the affairs of tourism, sighed as she glanced around the fields. The one where they stood seemed particularly wet, and Marshall lifted his foot to a squelching sound.

"Three days," she said. "I can have it open again in three days."

Marshall nodded, his muscles tight. It was almost five o'clock, and he'd had enough for one day. With nothing to eat and only stress on his plate, he surveyed the same land as Yuji. "All right. And what do you need to get the fields back to full production?"

"A dozen workers," she said. "We've already collected the slips and suckers from the front fifteen acres, but there's still a lot to do."

"Right." Marshall looked at her. "I'll get who I can. And I'll be here tomorrow in my work clothes. You can set me to task."

Yuji grinned, and Marshall's muscles bunched in anticipation of a hard day of work tomorrow. It was important to him to get out in the fields from time to time, and he could admit it had been quite a while since he'd last left his suit at home and donned a pair of jeans and a hat to keep the sun from burning him.

"And how did the greenhouses do?" He glanced behind the main building where they packaged and shipped their fruit. The long, white-paneled greenhouses glinted in the sun.

"Only one broken pane," Yuji said. "We've already fixed it."

"Good." So the majority of their slips and suckers for the new fields were intact. That was very good.

His phone buzzed, and he found Esther's name on it when he checked. *You're not at the northern plantation, are you?*

Fear squeezed his stomach and held on with an icy grip.

*Didn't I tell you?* he typed quickly, trying to remember if he actually had. They'd talked about his plantations last night at dinner, but his plans were so often fluid that he wasn't sure what he'd said.

*I have a truck and I'm at the Garden Grove fields.*

*Do you actually know how to drive a truck?*

Marshall chuckled and shook his head. *Of course I know how to drive.*

*Interesting.*

*I'll be here a while longer. Call you later?*

*No problem.* Half a minute passed and another message came in. *And you might try calling my personal number instead of work. Otherwise, you'll get a night driver. :)*

The next text included her number, and half of Marshall rejoiced while the other half quaked. Having her personal phone number felt like a step in the right direction toward a real relationship, and dang, if that didn't scare him off his own plantation.

# SEVEN

ESTHER ROLLED her neck from side to side and then slowly lowered her chin to her chest and leaned it back. Wow, it had been a long day. She'd checked her building after the storm, but because it was inland and along a major road, it had spared it from any damage. The worst thing was some extra trash, palm fronds, and leaves that had been blown in by the wind.

Her cars were safe in their garages, and nothing had been damaged. She'd checked in with all of her employees that morning too, and they had all been safe. Since she'd already canceled rides for the morning, she told her people she'd pay them to go work for the relief efforts on the island.

There were numerous homes along the beach that could use extra hands. Dozens of beachside businesses, like The Spam Hut and Two Coconuts, needed help getting everything cleaned out and put back together.

She'd contacted her afternoon appointments and

canceled all but two of them. After all, tourists did have to get to the airport to meet their flights. She'd been hoping to drive Marshall home, and maybe get an invite all the way inside his secret sanctum—his house. Just getting through the gate had taken years, so Esther wasn't sure why she thought she'd graduate to a guest in his home after only one dinner.

But he hadn't needed a ride anyway, and Esther turned on the bathtub with the hottest water she could stand. She usually drove around the island—a completely sedentary lifestyle—and today's hours of hard labor had her muscles in knots.

As she sank into the water and sighed, she let her eyes drift closed. Only forty-eight more hours to another date with Marshall, if he didn't cancel. Esther hated the doubts that existed in her mind. Why was she so insecure around him?

*Kaipo.*

*Akela.*

Those were the two big reasons Esther didn't think she had the capability to have a real relationship with a man. She'd shared so much in common with Kaipo, and one of their favorite activities had been snorkeling.

But with her head underwater, she couldn't have a conversation with him. She'd dated him for eight months and didn't even know his favorite color. When he'd broken up with her, he'd even said, "I barely know you."

Esther didn't miss him so much as she missed having *someone.* But Stacey had just gone through a horrific break-up with her fiancé, and they'd commiserated on the beach, gradually gathering more women around them until they had a whole club full of women who needed support, needed friendship, needed each other.

She reached for a towel and dried her hands before picking up her phone. She texted Stacey and said *I'm really nervous about going out with Marshall again.*

*Again?*

Esther's phone rang almost immediately after the text came in. She smiled as she swiped open the call from her best friend. "Hey, there. You survived the storm?"

"There's quite a bit of work to do in the gardens." Stacey sighed, and Esther imagined her pushing her red hair off her forehead. "But we have people, and…Fisher sent some help."

"Of course he did," Esther said suggestively.

"So when did you go out with Marshall?"

"Last night. We ate dinner at The Breezeway, since we were both staying at the hotel."

"Mm." That was it. No questions, and that was saying something for Stacey. She usually wanted to know what Esther had worn, and what she ate, and how things had gone. At least she used to, back when Esther used to go on dates.

"You know how I am." Esther didn't want to explain her nerves in so many words. Stacey already knew Esther, almost better than she knew herself.

"So you go slow," she said. "Marshall doesn't seem like one to rush into something anyway."

"What if he finds me boring?"

"Esther."

"Or too shallow?" The words built and built, almost drowning her. "Or what if we have nothing in common? I don't like chocolate in coffee, and he likes sashimi over sushi, and he's never been to Two Coconuts."

A beat of silence came through the line and then Stacey started laughing. "Okay, Esther. You've been to dinner in a very busy restaurant, with the threat of a storm hanging over you. Wait and see how things go when it's just back to island business as usual."

"He wore a designer pair of jeans to dinner last night."

This silence was new, and Esther didn't like it.

"That's not a deal-breaker," Stacey said.

Esther sunk a little lower in the water, getting her phone dangerously close to the citrus-scented bubbles. "We hate men who wear designer jeans."

"Did they have white stitching?"

Esther didn't want to answer, but she did. "Yes."

Stacey exhaled in one long hiss. "Okay, so he has a strike against him. Jeans can be burnt." She coughed, but Esther realized that she was laughing. A giggle crept up her throat too, and before she knew it, she and Stacey were laughing like Marshall's white-stitched jeans were the funniest thing on the planet.

"All right," Stacey said after she calmed down. "Seriously. Just be you. He'll like you."

Esther agreed just so she could get off the phone. She'd been herself for years, driving Marshall all over the island. And he'd never seen her. Never been interested. *She* hadn't been enough before, so what made her think a crossword puzzle book would suddenly up her value?

Thursday came faster than Esther could've imagined. Marshall had canceled his ride for Thursday and Friday, because he had that truck he claimed to know how to drive. He'd texted, not called, and said he'd be working in the fields for the next couple of days and didn't know what time he'd be available for dinner.

Esther met Jaylani at the office on Thursday morning, the round Hawaiian woman singing at the top of her lungs. She had a beautiful voice that should be in movies, and Esther smiled at her.

"Morning, Jay." Esther adjusted her purse on her shoulder.

"No Mister Robison this morning?" Jay turned and studied Esther as she stepped over to the board and updated the drivers and their jobs for the day. She wiped her name off Marshall for the next couple of days.

"Nope. He's apparently working at the plantations and has a truck of his own."

Jaylani twisted her long hair and piled it into a messy bun on the top of her head. She possessed a subtle beauty in the lines of her face, and Esther had never been able to feel anything but happiness around her.

Esther examined the board and saw that Jaylani's last drive was at one-thirty. "Could you take my last two jobs today?"

"You sure?" Jaylani stepped beside her and looked at the jobs. "Oh, one from the hotel to the airport, and a couple back. I can do that." She glanced at Esther. "You don't want to do it?"

Esther resisted the urge to rub her forehead. "I've got a headache, and if I can just get caught up on some paperwork today, I'll be ready to drive again tomorrow."

"Sure. Mahalo."

"Mahalo." Esther gave her a smile, the traditional word for *thank you* stumbling off her tongue. She left Jay looking at the board and went into her office. Without any driving jobs, Esther was free to get some payroll done, make sure they had their coupons ready for their upcoming Fourth of July promotion, and obsess about her date that night.

If it even happened.

She resisted the urge to check in with Marshall around lunchtime. She wasn't one-hundred percent sure what working in a pineapple field entailed, but she didn't think he'd have time to take a call and have a chat.

Instead, she found Jaylani in the small kitchen, heating up a container of food for lunch. "Jaylani, I wanted to talk to you about something."

"Sure thing." She turned and faced Esther, a quick smile filling her face. She was easily the best driver Esther employed, and her qualms about moving someone else into a management position waned.

"I was hoping you'd want to be my weekend manager," Esther said. With her early-morning schedule that wouldn't budge even when she could sleep in, she wanted someone else to take the weekend load.

"Really?"

"Fifty percent pay raise, and you'd get two other days off

during the week. I know your son has his surfing stuff on Thursdays."

"He does, yes." A smile filled Jaylani's whole face and she grabbed onto Esther's shoulders and kissed both of her cheeks. "I would love to do that. Sepa is old enough now to stay with the other boys on the weekends."

"You can bring them here," she said. "I don't need you to drive, but to manage the board, the drivers, the customers, the money."

Her dark eyes sparkled like inverse stars in the sky. "I can do it."

Of course she could. Esther smiled and nodded. "I'll start training you this weekend."

The afternoon hours dragged, with the chime on the door going off from time to time as her drivers came and went. When Esther couldn't take it anymore, she left the work she hadn't finished yet on her desk and got out of the office. Thankfully, she was able to make her escape when there wasn't anyone else to say good-bye to, and she went down Main Street and around the curve of the island toward her bungalow.

Her banana trees had taken a beating during the storm and she picked up a few more of the bigger leaves and branches. Anything to delay going into her empty house simply so she could stare at her silent phone, hoping Marshall would text or call.

She puttered around the yard in her slacks, finally going in to change into her bathing suit. There were still a few hours left before dinner time, and Esther wanted to spend them in her favorite place: the beach.

So she grabbed her beach bag, which was always stocked with tanning lotion, an extra pair of sunglasses, a bag of her favorite dried mango, and several tubes of Chapstick. She changed, snagged a big, floppy hat from the hook and a water bottle from the fridge and stepped out her back door.

She didn't live right on the beach, but a close three-minute walk. So five minutes later, she had her blue and white striped towel spread on the sand, her toes curling into the warmth of the shore as she tipped her face toward the sun.

A measure of peace and relaxation she couldn't find anywhere else seeped into her, the same way the sun soaked into her skin. She knew Stacey wouldn't be able to get away for an hour of sunbathing, but Tawny probably could.

She taught beach yoga classes, and she'd just signed a contract with Sweet Breeze. In fact, she'd given Esther the idea to send Fisher DuPont a proposal for Your Ride. She hadn't because she wanted to remain loyal to Stacey.

But Tawny had said, "But you've got to do what's best for you too, right?" She'd shrugged and sipped her bright blue pineapple and blue raspberry soda, which made the naturalist in Esther recoil.

She sent a quick text to Tawny and started slathering her skin with lotion so she didn't get burned.

*Be right there!* Tawny's enthusiastic text brought a smile to Esther's face. Sure enough, only fifteen minutes later, Tawny opened her beach chair and said, "It's amazing how a storm blew through only two days ago." She stood next to her chair and gazed out at the bay. "You'd never know it."

Crews had obviously worked hard—and probably

through the night—to get the beach cleaned up. Which made sense. Getaway Bay was famous for its beaches. They were why people saved for years and spent small fortunes to come to this private, pristine, tucked away part of Hawaii.

Tawny took a bottle from her beach bag and spritzed the lightener into her hair before tossing it over her bare shoulders. She wore a strapless bikini the color of limes, with a cover up over that. Since she worked outside for hours each morning, she didn't really need the additional time in the sun to get tan. But she did want her brown hair to get some streaks in it.

She called it mousy, but Esther had never thought of it like that. She grinned up at her friend as she got everything settled. "I can't stay long," Esther said.

"No problem." Tawny finally sat down in the chair and extended her long legs out in front of her, blowing a sigh from between her lips. "I only need an hour away anyway."

"Away?" Esther repeated. "Tough day?"

"I'm in training to be a Crossfit instructor," she said, grimacing like Crossfit was a swear word. But she loved the stuff. "And it's kicking my butt."

"Well, your butt's looking great." Esther should probably get into something like yoga or Crossfit, but she preferred her treadmill and her favorite TV shows on repeat.

Tawny laughed and reached for her soda. Bright red liquid colored the straw, indicating she was on her cherry limeade kick. "So did you get the contracts from Sweet Breeze?"

"Owen said they were signed, but I haven't seen them yet."

"Have you told Stacey?"

Esther reached for her water bottle, giving herself a moment to formulate an answer. "Stacey's dating Fisher. I'm sure she'll be fine with it."

Tawny's eyes flew open and she almost dumped her soda in the sand. "She's *dating* him?"

Esther shrugged. "I think so." She didn't want to give away all of Stacey's secrets, and it had only been a few days since their last Beach Club meeting, where Stacey had mentioned her lunch date with Fisher.

Tawny's mouth stayed open for another couple of seconds, and Esther could practically feel her despair. "What about you?" Esther asked. "Any hunky men showing up to beach yoga?"

She pressed her lips together and shook her head. "My idea for a male-centric class hasn't gone as well as I'd hoped."

"You mean women don't want their husbands and boyfriends out on the beach with a hot brunette." Esther threw Tawny a smile. "While she wears almost nothing and twists her body into strange shapes."

Tawny rolled her eyes, but whether it was about the hot brunette part or the twisty part, Esther wasn't sure.

"Men don't really take vacations together, do they?" Tawny sucked on her straw, and Esther took another long drink of her water too.

"Not really." She rolled over onto her back and turned her face away from Tawny. "I have something to tell you."

"Oh, yeah?"

"Will you do my back first?"

Tawny's hands landed on Esther's back, smoothing the lotion on for a few seconds in silence. "Okay, what?"

"I'm sort of seeing someone too."

"You are?" Tawny's voice could've called dogs. A lot of dogs. "Great. Just great. Everyone is going to end up in wedded bliss, and I'll still be doing downward dog at the freaking crack of dawn." The anger in her voice didn't fall on deaf ears, and Esther switched position so she was facing Tawny.

"I've had one date with the guy. We're a long way from 'wedded bliss'." Esther tried to give her a big smile. "Besides, you'll meet someone."

Tawny's jaw tightened and released. Tightened and released. "I'd like that." Her muscles unclenched, and Esther kept an eye on her from behind the mirrored sunglasses. "I think it's a little ironic that the two most stubborn women have started dating someone."

"I'm not stubborn," Esther protested.

"You've been adamant about remaining single." Tawny removed a bag of potato chips from her bag, and Esther sat right back up, hoping for a handful of the salty snack. "You and Stacey both. And now she's dating a billionaire. Who are you going out with? His general manager?"

Esther swallowed, her eyes migrating from the chips to Tawny's face. "Uh, his best friend?" Why she phrased it as a question, she wasn't sure.

"Marshall?" Tawny dropped the chips in the sand, her eyes going as round as dinner plates. "You've been in love with him forever!"

Esther glanced down the beach, though it was deserted. "I have not."

"Years."

"Only two. That barely counts as plural." Esther hated that she hadn't been able to get over her crush on the pineapple god.

"Are you still driving him?"

"Sometimes," she said evasively. "He's been busy because of the storm." But all at once, a wall of doubt slammed into her mind. Maybe he didn't want her to drive him anymore. Maybe she'd lose him as a client. Maybe he didn't really know how to drive a truck.

"Well." Tawny took out a handful of chips before passing the bag to Esther. "I hope he's good to you. I hope it works out."

And Esther knew that she really meant it.

Esther nodded and managed to say, "Thanks, Tawny. I'll help you find a hot, yoga-loving man," before her attention drifted back to the water lapping the shore. She didn't like the swirling doubts in her mind, and she hated the well of insecurity that never seemed to run dry.

# EIGHT

MARSHALL EASED the rental car into a hard-packed dirt driveway, wondering if he had the right place. He'd stayed too long at the plantation, but it felt good to get his muscles moving and be with his employees as they worked to plant new suckers and slips.

Esther said she lived in a little bungalow on the beach, and he relaxed when he caught sight of a sign on her mailbox that said Pinnett. So this was it.

The front yard had three chickens pecking in it, and she'd never struck him as the type of woman to house fowl, gather eggs, or put up with feathers.

Before he had the black SUV in park, the front door opened, and the most gorgeous woman he'd ever seen walked out. Esther's hair curled over her shoulders, and she wore a bright blue dress that narrowed at her waist and flared at her knees. The bodice hugged all her curves and showed off her tanned arms and shoulders.

He slammed on the brake, jerking the car to a stop. A smile exploded onto Esther's face and she stepped across the lawn in a pair of white sandals, her laughter meeting his ears even through the closed windows.

Marshall swallowed and flipped the gearshift into park before getting out of the car. "What?" he asked.

"I think I should drive." She paused out of his reach, and every cell in his body mourned the fact that he couldn't trail his fingers up her arm, through that hair, and down her neck right before he kissed her.

He cleared his throat, sending the thoughts to the back of his mind for him to deal with later. The attraction between him and Esther felt like it had always been there but had just now been activated somehow.

*How?* he wondered. Why hadn't he felt it before?

"You look nice," she said.

Marshall looked down at what he was wearing, because somehow his mind wasn't working right. Khaki shorts. Blue button down. Loafers with no socks. Casual. Easy. How he hoped tonight's dinner would go. "Thanks. You look...stunning." He took a few steps toward her and put both hands on her shoulders, ran them down her arms and took both hands in his. "Amazing. Beautiful."

She smiled up at him, and the easiness he'd been hoping for filtered into his system, allowing him to grin back. "So I thought we'd do something a little...off the beaten path for dinner tonight?"

Esther fixed him with a look that was part flirt and part seriousness. "What does that mean, exactly?"

"I have a catamaran, and I thought we'd sail out a bit and eat on the water."

Esther's eyebrows went up and she stiffened in front of him. "Sailing?"

"You don't like boats?"

"No, I...I love boats, actually." A smile landed on her face, and a measure of relief spread through Marshall. "Sailing sounds nice."

"Good." Because he'd already ordered the food and it would be at the docks at about the same time they would. He checked his phone. "Well, we should get going then. The daylight fades fast."

"Well, if *someone* hadn't worked until six o'clock." She bumped him with her hip and sauntered around the front of the SUV. He chuckled as she did, the soft scent of her getting under his skin. She smelled like sunshine and lotion, and he couldn't get enough of her.

He held her door while she got in the car, and then he quickly went around to the driver's seat. "This is weird," he said as he turned the key in the ignition. He flashed her a smile. "Right?"

She rolled her window down and ran her fingers through her hair. "I like it."

Which meant Marshall would drive her anywhere, whenever she wanted. He kept those feelings close to his heart, buried beneath his tongue, as he navigated out of the bay and down the shore to the dock.

Sure enough, the pizza van waited right where he'd asked them to, and he eased the SUV to a stop beside it.

"Pizza?" Esther asked, eyeing the van.

"Don't tell me you don't eat pizza." Horror washed through Marshall. He wouldn't end things with her over this very wrong dietary choice, but well, he'd ended relationships for less. Just the thought of being in a relationship had him twitching and wishing he could get on the catamaran and sail away for good.

*Stop it*, he told himself. He had no reason to believe Esther was here for anything but her interest in him. Him. Not his money. Not his plantations. Just him.

"Of course I eat pizza." Esther opened her door and started to get out. "It just doesn't seem like billionaire fare."

"Oh yeah," Marshall said as he turned off the car and got out too. "Pizza is the preference of billionaires from here to the mainland."

"There's basically ocean from here to the mainland." Esther shook her head and smiled. She linked her arm through his when she met him at the corner of the SUV. "I hope you got something with olives. I love olives."

"Loves olives. Noted." He hoped she'd laugh, but her phone had distracted her. She glanced at it, a frown pulling between her eyes.

"I need to make a call real quick." She stepped away, her business face on. He only heard, "An accident? Jaylani, what's...?" before the wind swept her voice away.

He paid the pizza guy for the pizzas, salad, and sodas and mimed to her that he was going to take the food onto the boat. She nodded, a half-look of disgust on her face. He knew that face. It meant she was getting news she didn't like and didn't want to deal with. Marshall made that face ten times a day.

But he walked away from her, hoping harder with every step that she wouldn't have to cancel. That he'd get to see her standing at the helm, her hair blowing gloriously in the wind. That he'd get to hold her hand, and maybe, just maybe, get to kiss her goodnight.

Thankfully, she joined him in the galley only five minutes later, her phone stashed out of sight. "Sorry," she said. "Emergency on the night crew."

"You have a night crew?" Marshall had meant to find out more about her car service, something he usually did when he hired someone. But his mother had signed him up, and he'd simply taken over paying the bill every month.

"Of course." Esther gave him a look out of the corner of her eye. "I'm open twenty-four hours a day, seven days a week."

"You are?" For some reason, that surprised Marshall. "Why?"

Her glare was definitely full of annoyance now. "Because I want to be the only full service car service, day or night, on the island. Everyone else closes. We don't." She tapped the pizza box. "Can we eat now? Or did you get me out on this boat to talk business?"

"I know a lot about business," Marshall said, a stitch starting in his chest and radiating down his arms. By the angry glint in her eyes and the tight pinch against her mouth, she didn't want him to give her business advice. "But let's sail out before we eat."

"Fine." She turned and marched outside, where she sat on the bench seat under the shade.

*Fix this*, Marshall told himself as he grabbed a can of cola and followed her. He was the ultimate fixer in the Robison family. If something went wrong on the plantations, he fixed it. If his family needed something, or had a problem, he had a solution.

But as he watched Esther put her shades on, effectively shutting him out, he wondered if he'd be able to fix her.

He shook the thoughts from his brain. She wouldn't like him thinking she was broken, or that there was something wrong with her because she didn't want his unsolicited business advice. So he shelved his pride and sat next to her.

"Sorry." He popped the top on his can. "Your business is none of my business."

She visibly deflated, and Marshall wanted to know what had gotten her all riled up in the first place.

"Want to tell me about it?" he asked, signaling the pilot of the yacht that yes, they were ready. Esther had just taken a deep breath when the boat started to move. She yelped and grabbed onto his arm with five fingers that felt like vices.

"Whoa," he said. "We're just setting out. It'll be slow at first. You're fine."

"Who's driving the boat?"

"My pilot."

"Your pilot," she repeated like she didn't believe him.

"Sometimes I sail," he said. "But I didn't want to be up in the captain's chair when I could be down here with you." He hoped that would be romantic enough to get her talking. He took a long drink of the carbonated drink, grateful for the burn down his throat.

She said nothing for a minute or two, and Marshall was

just gearing himself up to ask her a very personal question when she blurted, "What is this, Marshall?"

He gestured to the water rushing by at a faster clip now. "The ocean. A boat. Sailing. Dinner."

"It's a date."

"That too."

"Are we dating?"

Marshall's chest collapsed, but he managed to take another breath and another drink. "I'm a bit rusty, but I think when two people go out more than once, it can be considered dating." He focused on her, hoping she could see more than what he'd said. Feel more of what he felt.

"Yeah, you don't go out with anyone twice."

"Clearly, that's false." He swept one arm around her. "You've made me break my rules."

"I wasn't aware of your rules."

Marshall scoffed. "First, yes, you were. And second, you're not a very good liar." He added a chuckle to the statement so she wouldn't find his words too harsh.

She leaned into his body a little bit, but that could've been from the new direction the boat took. No matter what, he'd take it. He liked the nearness of her when other women had been barely tolerable. He liked talking to her when other conversations had been insufferable noise.

"So tell me the rules," she said.

"I have a lot of work functions I'm required to attend," he said. "The rules are quite simple. Take a different woman to each one. That way, there are no attachments, there are no hurt feelings, and there are no…." He paused, not quite sure he should say the last part.

"Relationships," Esther said for him. "Why didn't you want a relationship? I mean, maybe you still don't."

"Why have you never dated?"

"Who says I've never dated?" She turned her head to look at him, and he could've dived into her blue eyes and stayed for a good, long while. Not only that, but her mouth was dangerously close now, and all Marshall could do was think about kissing her.

"Marshall?"

"Hm?" He straightened and pulled himself out of his fantasies. "Oh, uh, I may have asked around a little."

"Asked around a little?" She didn't sound happy about his espionage.

He added, "I just asked Stacey. She said you hadn't been out with anyone in a while. That's all."

Esther blinked a couple of times. "I can't believe she told you that."

"It was all very casual," he said. "A text. It was nothing."

"Nothing." Esther scoffed and looked out over the water again. "Why don't you date?" she asked again.

"It's complicated," he said. "I haven't had the best of luck in the past, and I suppose I became jaded."

"Oh, that's a lame explanation." She gave a light laugh, but it was clear she wanted more. More details. More of a reason.

The boat started to slow as Marshall tried to find the words. "Yeah." He exhaled. "So, the short version is, I fell in love with a woman named Lorna. We got married. Two months later, I discovered her money laundering operation from the third floor of my Garden Grove facility."

His emotions went up and down with every swell of water as he waited for Esther to respond.

"Wow." She sighed. "That sucks."

For some reason, he laughed. The sound was full of freedom, something Marshall hadn't felt since meeting Lorna all those years ago. "You're right. It did suck. She only got away with about three hundred thousand, and she's in jail now. So." He lifted one shoulder in a shrug, though the whole ordeal had cost him a lot more than money.

"Divorced then?"

"Yep."

"And thinking every woman is like Lorna."

"Yeah—no. I mean...." He pulled her closer and ducked his mouth closer to her ear. "I guess, maybe. Until you."

She snuggled into him, which only made Marshall's blood pump a little faster. "Why me?"

Marshall didn't think about it this time. He just vocalized what came to him. "Because I've known you for a long time, and you've never made a move. Because you already have your own money. Because you're...you."

Esther twisted in his arms, her blue eyes brighter than he'd ever seen them. "Me?"

"You," he repeated, unsure of exactly why the attraction had started between them, but very glad it had.

She leaned further into him, her eyes drifting halfway closed and her mouth just begging him to kiss it.

So he did.

# NINE

ESTHER HAD DREAMED of kissing Marshall Robison every day and every night for the past seven hundred and thirty days. Maybe seven hundred and thirty-one, if last year was Leap Year, which she couldn't really remember, because she was *kissing Marshall Robison.*

And it didn't matter that the man hadn't gone on a second date in years. He still knew how to kiss a woman like he meant it, and wow, did he mean it.

Esther breathed in the citrus and soil scent of him, threaded her fingers through his hair, and kept him right against her mouth.

The boat rocked underneath her when he finally broke the connection between them. He leaned his forehead against hers and said, "All right. I definitely think we're dating now."

And while Esther had not appreciated his business advice, nor the fact that he'd asked her best friend about her dating history, she sure did like Marshall. A quiet giggle came out of her mouth, and she said, "I hope so."

Part of her worries had evaporated during the kiss. The part that wondered whether he was just a jerk and that was why he didn't date anyone. Not because of them, but because of him.

But he was kind, hard-working, smart. He was every-thing she'd hoped he'd be if she could just get to know him for more than the stoic billionaire who rode in the backseat of her car twice a day.

She drew her knees to her chest and leaned fully into his body now. "I haven't dated for a while because my last couple of boyfriends didn't really seem interested in me. I...." She wasn't sure she could reveal this much of herself so soon. It seemed impossible that only five days had passed since she'd given him the crossword puzzle book.

"Hey, how was your birthday?"

"Great. Fine." The wooden tone to his voice said differently.

"You didn't even celebrate it, did you?"

"What's to celebrate?" He shifted behind her, the only indication that he didn't like this conversation. "One year older. Still alive."

"And at your age, that's a real accomplishment," she quipped.

A beat passed with only the splashing of water against the sides of the boat. Then he filled the air with his booming laughter. "Oh, I like you, Esther."

Esther felt warm inside and out, and she said, "I'll make you a cake. You'll come over tomorrow and I'll sing to you.

You can't just let your thirty-eighth birthday go by with nothing."

His thumb traced a pattern over her forearm. "How did you know how old I am?"

Esther swallowed her fear, and all her inhibitions. "I'm a very observant person. And I hear a lot of conversations in my car. And I've...had a crush on you for two years." She said the last part in a huge rush, hoping he'd overlook them.

More silence, the ocean waters that usually soothed her only sort of doing their usual job. Marshall kept breathing steadily, in then out.

"Why didn't your last couple of boyfriends seem interested in you?"

So he wasn't going to let it go. Esther thought about turning around and kissing him again, distracting him so she wouldn't have to answer.

"Honestly?" she asked.

"I would hope we'd always be honest with each other." His voice hummed through her body, low and deep, almost like a purr.

"One called me shallow," Esther said. "The other said he didn't even know me. For a while there, I thought I was incapable of making a connection with a man." She still thought that, even now. Today. Right here on this forty-five-foot catamaran. She tried to shrug, like this conversation wasn't stabby, didn't puncture her lungs when she talked about it. But with his arms around her, her shoulders couldn't lift too far.

"So I put on my business suits and my heels and I drive rich people around the island," she said. "I listen, and I pay attention. I give advice if they ask for it. I know all the best places off the beaten path to eat, and if you want the best pedicure in town, I know where to drop you off."

"A pedicure? Wow. I think I'll pass on that one." He somehow drew her closer as he breathed out, and she closed her eyes, the salty sea breeze and the sound of the waves creating a sense of serenity she never wanted to release.

But her night did get better with one single word. "Pizza?"

———

Esther woke at five o'clock the next morning, despite her late arrival back at her bungalow. She lay in bed, the soft sheets cool in the morning breeze that came through the crack in the window.

If she breathed in deep enough, she could still smell Marshall's cologne on her skin. Still feel the gentle and then insistent press of his mouth against hers as he kissed her goodnight. She hadn't had a man walk her to her front door and kiss her since high school, and she felt a little giddy at the thought of seeing him again.

But not that morning. He still had his work truck, and he'd be spending another day in the Garden Grove plantation on the south side of the island. She liked that his hands were a little rougher because of his work. She liked listening to him talk about how pineapple plants were cultivated, harvested, and replanted. She really liked that he'd sauntered back toward his car, and then turned back. Came back. Pressed her against the door with the words, "One more kiss," before kissing her so completely she'd had to stay leaning against the door while he climbed in the SUV and backed down her dirt lane.

She touched her lips, almost expecting them to be swollen, bruised. A smile flitted across them, and she finally pushed herself up. Though she wasn't driving Marshall this morning, she knew she wouldn't be able to sleep in.

She did take more time to get ready than she normally did, but the routine didn't vary. She put on her oils, took her vitamins and supplements, and adorned herself with expensive silk suits and jewels in her ears.

When she showed up at her parents airy home higher in the hills of the island, her mom looked up from her morning coffee, the blonde hair Esther had inherited from her recently cut.

"Esther." Her mom's face bloomed with happiness, and she left her laptop and came to embrace Esther.

"Hey, Mom. What're you doing?" She nodded toward the computer and sipped her caramel coffee.

"Oh, we finally got down to Yukijama's. I'm doing a food critique for the paper."

"You went without me?" Esther smiled so her mom would know it was a joke. She hadn't wanted to go to the new authentic Japanese restaurant that had just gone in on the northern tip of the island, but her mom got paid to write reviews of all things food. Being one of the best cooks on the planet had certain perks.

"It was good," her mom said. "I think even you would've liked it."

Esther made a face and shook her head.

"You're not working today?"

"My usual morning client canceled for the week." Actually, Esther needed to check with Marshall and see if he'd be going into the office over the weekend. She suspected that yes, he would. He sometimes worked seven days a week when there hadn't been a huge storm that had affected his entire operation.

She pulled out her phone and sent him a quick text, remembering why she'd been too busy to ask him last night. They hadn't talked about work or business at all after they'd started talking about their relationship. Esther was glad. She didn't need his advice for how to run Your Ride. She'd built it from the ground up, with just a car she couldn't afford and a used pair of black heels.

Plus, there had been all that kissing....

Esther felt heated just thinking about it, and when his name popped up on her screen, she almost had to fan herself. *Yes, I'll be working all weekend. What about you?*

*What about me?* She smiled at her message, hoping it was flirty and fun. *What do you mean?*

*What are you doing this weekend? If you're not busy, maybe you'd like to hang out with me.*

Esther's thumbs couldn't fly fast enough over the screen. *While you work?*

*Yeah. I'll order whatever you want for lunch. You name it.*

Oh, he was what she wanted, and she almost put that in a text. But her mom swiped her phone away and asked, "Who are you texting?" She scanned the messages in the two heartbeats it took Esther to realize what was happening.

"I've been talking to you and you haven't heard a word." Her mom looked up and met her eyes. "Who's Marshall?"

"My...boyfriend," Esther said, a small earthquake shaking her insides. "We just started dating yesterday."

Her mom smiled as she returned her focus to the phone. "That's great, honey. He's your client?"

Esther cleared her throat and took another sip of her coffee, but it tasted too sweet now. And it was way too cold. She dumped the remaining bit down the drain and took a few moments to throw the cup in the recycling bin. "Uh, yeah. I've been driving him to his pineapple plantations for a few years now."

Seven years. But her mom didn't need to know the semantics. It wasn't like Esther had been crushing on him all that time.

"Hm." Her mother handed the phone back, and Esther didn't like the guttural hum. It means her mom disapproved.

"Where's Dad?" she asked instead. She felt she should get a party, a great big chocolate cake, something for dating again. Surely her mom knew it had been a while for Esther. Or maybe not. After Sean's death, her mom had become half the person she'd been when he'd been alive. It was as if a piece of her had gone with him when he'd passed away.

Settling behind the laptop again, she said, "He's out in the orchard." She focused back on the screen and added, "Do you and George want to do Sunday brunch this weekend?"

Esther had no idea what her brother would be doing on Sunday morning, but she promised to ask and let her mom know before escaping out the back door. She breathed in the air here, higher up on the island, away from the beach. Green trees and pale sand stretched out before her before meeting bright blue water, and she drank in the glorious sight. She really did love Hawaii.

She found her father on a ladder, gathering limes from one of his dozen trees. He saw her coming and climbed down, depositing his harvest in a basket before walking toward her with a big smile on his face.

"Esther." He drew her into a hug, and she loved the way she felt safe and adored within the circle of his arms.

She sighed out her frustration with her mom and held onto him tight. He was tall and broad, and when he stepped back, he wore his usual happiness in the twinkle of his bright blue eyes.

"Limes are on?" she asked, nodding toward the trees.

"First harvest." He went back to the ladder and climbed back up. "I'll hand them to you."

She let him pass the green-skinned fruit down to her, and they just kept coming. "Are you going to take them to the farmer's market?" she asked.

"Tomorrow morning. I've got papayas and mangos to pick too." He sounded absolutely gleeful, and Esther couldn't help smiling as she shook her head and kept piling limes into the basket.

But she loved that he had something that made him happy. After Sean's death, he hadn't fallen into an abyss the way her mom had. And while he'd relocated the family to Hawaii, he kept pictures of Sean around the house, spoke of him often, and never shied away from a hard conversation.

Which made him the perfect person for Esther to talk to about Marshall.

"Dad?" she asked as he climbed down and moved the ladder to a mango tree nearby.

"What, bug?" He seemed to know she needed more attention from him than he could give perched ten feet in the air, picking juicy mangos. Watching her, he cocked his head slightly to the side. "What is it?"

"I started dating someone," she said.

His face brightened and he grinned. "That's great, Esther. You haven't been out with anyone in a while."

She nodded and gestured for him to go up the ladder. He did, and as he passed down bigger, heavier mangos for her to layer in a box, she said, "Right. And I like him, but well, he's a client."

"Of yours?"

"Yeah, I drive him where he needs to go every day." Another mango. Another.

"You think this might be a problem?"

"I don't know."

"Obviously, you do," he said. "Or you wouldn't be talking to me about it."

"Maybe I just need someone to tell me it isn't a problem."

Her dad sighed, finished the tree, and put both feet on solid ground again. He looked at her, and those blue eyes popped with energy. "I can't tell you that. Only you can decide that for yourself."

"Mom thinks it's unprofessional."

"She said that?" His eyebrows went sky high.

"Not in words." Esther mimicked her mom and made the deep humming sound in her throat.

Her dad laughed and set about moving the ladder to another tree. "Does he have a problem with it?"

"Doesn't seem to."

"Do you?"

"I like him," she repeated. "I have for a while." As if that somehow made their relationship okay. But Esther didn't want to break up with him. And he was her best client. She didn't want him to hire another service either.

"Maybe this is something you play by ear." He bent to pick up the nearly full box, a groan seeping from his throat. "Wow, I'm not as young as I used to be." He chuckled, and Esther grabbed the basket of limes and went with him to the shed where he'd polish up the fruit before taking it to the farmer's market in the morning.

"Thanks, Dad." She gave him a peck on the cheek. "I have to get to work. It was good to see you."

"Bye, bug. Let me know how it goes with your boyfriend!"

She waved to indicate that she would. She wouldn't be able to hide it. No matter what happened—good or bad—her dad would know. She'd either end up engaged, or she'd be back in the orchard at some point, crying and seeking comfort after Marshall broke her heart.

# TEN

MARSHALL PUSHED the treadmill to go faster, hoping he could keep up. He'd been running for forty minutes, and he probably should stop before he blew out a knee. Now that he was thirty-eight, high-impact exercise had real risks.

He'd begged out of a cake party at Esther's last night, citing a sore back and aching arms. Sorting suckers and planting slips was no job for the weak, as Marshall had learned the hard way. But Esther would be joining him at his office today, and she'd promised to bring the cake with his usual morning coffee.

They were getting a late start to the morning, but Marshall had been up at his usual early hour. He was glad the boards were gone from his windows, and that nothing around his property had been too badly damaged. He'd lost the patio set he'd really liked, but somehow Popoki still found his way into Marshall's house at will.

He emerged from his bedroom, freshly showered and

shaved, to find the feline balled up on his kitchen counter. The first several times the cat had gotten in and made himself at home, Marshall had been startled. But now he just ran his fingers down the gray fur on the cat's back and said, "Morning, cat."

Popoki didn't purr, and Marshall had listened to his neighbor tell him that the cat was too old, that his vocal chords had gone out. Marshall wasn't sure if he believed the older man, but Popoki just squinted his eyes in bliss at the pat, but no purr sounded in his throat.

Marshall could make exactly one thing in his kitchen: coffee. So while Esther would have a cup for him, he wasn't expecting her for another two hours, and he needed some caffeine to convince his body that yes, it was morning, and no, exercise would not kill them.

Not-his-cat followed him outside to the patio, where Marshall sat on the flagstones to sip his beverage. The wind whipped up, causing the sound of rustling and whispers to fly through the air. Marshall loved the way the earth talked to the wind, and how the air responded. He loved that he could hear the sound of the waves crashing against the lava rock far below. And he loved that he'd get to spend the day with Esther, even if she did come with cake and wanted to celebrate his birthday.

*Gonna have to tell her*, he thought as he got up and went back inside to really get ready for the day. He couldn't go to the office in gym shorts and a T-shirt that hadn't been laundered in too long. There would be a lot of people in the building today, as the clean up was still in progress at all four plantations.

He had temporary work permits to file, and the seasonal paychecks to cut, as he'd promised everyone they'd get paid weekly for their labors. He needed them now, and he needed them to come back in the future if he needed to quickly hire a slew of workers.

So he wouldn't miss his deadlines, nor break his promises. He put on a dark brown suit his father had chosen for him and slipped into a pair of leather shoes that he'd bought on his last trip to Italy.

He wondered if Esther could ever leave Your Ride and travel the world with him. He didn't leave Hawaii all that often, but he had taken trips to Costa Rica, Brazil, the Philippines, and Thailand to visit other high-producing plantations. He'd spoken to their foremen, learned some things he didn't know, toured their facilities and fields, and taken what he could and applied it to the Robison empire on the islands here.

Contrary to popular belief, Marshall did vacation sometimes, and he knew how to relax, as evidenced by the time he spent on his catamaran. He was sure Esther didn't know and hadn't observed that about him, and he wanted her to know. Wanted her to see.

He wasn't sure what kind of men she'd dated previously, but she was the least shallow woman he knew. Maybe that wasn't saying much, because all of his previous dates had been giggly, grinning females who just wanted to be in the forefront of any pictures that were taken.

He gathered his work together and put it in his briefcase, glancing out the window as Esther pulled into his driveway.

A smile danced across his face, and he ducked his head as if she'd be able to see it.

Marshall wasn't quite sure when he'd felt this happy, and he wanted to hold onto the feeling as long as possible. So when Esther got out of the car and took up her position near the back door, he decided that behavior had to stop.

He moved to the front door and opened it, calling, "You want to come in for a minute? I'm not quite ready." A lie. A big, fat lie. His tie was precisely knotted. Jacket buttoned. Briefcase packed.

But he didn't want his girlfriend to act like his chauffeur. Problem was, Esther was both his chauffeur *and* his girlfriend.

An internal struggle began, and Marshall had no idea how it would end. Esther moved toward him, her heels clicking delicately against the pavers as she mounted the steps.

He leaned into the doorway, his arms crossed, hoping she'd relax a little. "Morning." He hadn't seen her at all yesterday, and he'd been tortured with the memory of that last kiss, with her pressed against her door and drinking him in like she was dying of thirst.

He licked his lips and reached for her as soon as she was within arm's length. A giggle of surprise burst from her, and he spun her around before kissing her against the other half of his front door.

She managed to separate her lips from his for a beat, long enough to breathe, "Marshall," in a way that only encouraged him.

"Hmm?" He moved his mouth to her neck, because if she wanted to talk, she should be able to.

"I thought you just needed a ride."

"I do." She smelled like limes and fresh air, and he nosed her earlobe before nipping it with his teeth. She stiffened and he almost pulled back, but then she melted right into his arms, running those delicious fingernails along his neck and into his hair.

He kissed her again, knowing he wouldn't be able to at the office. Everyone would be buzzing about her being there anyway, but he'd already decided he didn't care. She'd said she could bring some work of her own to do, and while he didn't taste any frosting on her lips, he was sure the cake would make an appearance at some point today.

He finally got control of himself and pulled away. After clearing his throat, he said, "All right. That was the best greeting I've had in a while." He kept his hand in hers as he led her into the house. "You want the grand tour now, or later?"

"The cake will probably melt in the car." She glanced around, though, like she wanted to see all the intimate places Marshall lived. Problem was, that wasn't prevalent in this house. He spent most of his time in his office, or at Fisher's hotel. He really only slept here, worked out here, and fed Popoki here.

"Later, then," he said, glad he could avoid leading her all over his stark space. He collected his briefcase and went to the car with her. He made a grab for the door handle and opened it himself before she could do it.

Her lips pursed, and he said, "Remember how I'm doing this now?"

She stepped back and folded her arms. "I don't think you should pay me then."

He scoffed and lowered himself into the car. "Of course I'm going to pay you."

She walked around the front of the vehicle, clearly unhappy. With both doors closed, and both of her hands on the wheel, she should've been able to go. But she didn't. The smell of chocolate and caramel and coffee mixed into a tantalizing scent that made his mouth water.

"Half," she finally said. "You can pay me half."

"That's ridiculous."

"I'm *your ride*," she said.

"I know what you are," he said coolly. "If you insist on defining what it's worth to open a car door for someone, you'll have to let me do some research for the going rate of such things."

She scoffed so loud, it sounded like she was choking. "Going rate? What are you going to do? Google it?"

"Exactly."

"Exactly what?"

Marshall shouldn't be enjoying this teensy tiff so much, but he really was. "Esther," he said softly. "I simply don't want you to open my door or make me ride in the back. If it bothers you that much, I'll pay you ten percent less for the car service. But it doesn't bother me, and I like getting picked up my girlfriend."

Several beats of silence passed before she finally put the

car in gear and started around his circular driveway. "Fifteen percent."

"Five."

"You just said ten!" She swatted him, and he yanked his arm away, chuckling.

"Six," he said.

She pressed her lips together, but the smile still curved them a bit. "Fine, ten percent."

"If you insist."

"I do." She expertly maneuvered the car down the mountain, the atmosphere between them charged but casual. As she pulled into the parking lot, and he instructed her to go around back to park, his nerves began a riot.

She'd want to bring that cake in, sing to him—*maybe in front of everyone,* he thought with horror—and then get to work.

He put his hand on her arm and looked at her.

She watched him back, searching his expression for something he probably wasn't showing on his face.

"I have to tell you something."

She put the car in park but left the engine idling, like she might just drop him off and go, depending on what he said.

"There's a reason I don't like celebrating my birthday."

"Okay." She held very still, and Marshall liked that she listened. Watched. Didn't jump to conclusions or freak out.

"It was my birthday—my thirtieth, the big three-oh—when I found out about Lorna's scheme." His words started to turn hollow as his memories took him back to that place, but he pulled himself back to this moment. This moment with Esther.

"I'd gone to the Garden Grove plantation to surprise her. See, I was supposed to be in Costa Rica, but I'd come home early so we could be together." He removed his hand from Esther and looked out the windshield. After another breath, he felt strong enough to go on.

"There was no chocolate cake. Just ledgers of her illegal activity. I left that office and moved up here, and a couple of days later, my mother got me the free trial to your car service." He wondered now if there had been some sort of divine intervention. If so, waiting eight years for it to come to fruition seemed cruel.

"I've only been driving you for seven years," she said.

Esther, ever the queen of details. Marshall loved that about her, and he didn't resist the temptation to reach out and tuck her hair behind her ear. "Your hair isn't in a pony-tail." He'd just noticed, though he'd definitely had his hands in her hair while he kissed her.

"It was when I got to your house," she said, quirking one eyebrow at him.

Heat traveled through his core and into his face. "Sorry."

"Nothing to be sorry about," she said in a near whisper. "I'm sorry about Lorna. But maybe we can replace your bad birthday memory with some good ones."

He nodded, the whole story almost out. "I didn't use your service for a few months. Maybe longer. I don't really remember when I started, because I thought it was kind of absurd that me, a big, brawny billionaire, couldn't drive himself to work." He chuckled, the sound light so the moment wouldn't become too heavy.

He looked right into Esther's brilliant blue eyes, glad

when he saw the flint of attraction burning there. "But I'm glad I did."

"Me too." She leaned forward and gave him a chaste kiss over the console. "I mean, big, brawny, billionaires need help sometimes too, right?"

He laughed, and the sound of her joining in with him made a new birthday memory he wanted to hold onto for a long time. "Right," he said, before kissing her again, this time not quite so chaste.

# ELEVEN

ESTHER GRIPPED her bag with more force than necessary to keep it in her hand. While Marshall had never said the office would be empty, she'd sort of assumed it would be. But activity buzzed everywhere she looked, and at least a dozen people worked at desks and stood at a water cooler when she walked in.

Marshall nodded to them, said hello, introduced her to a few people whose names she catalogued for later in case she needed them. They finally made it to the fourth floor, where a sprawling office housed an enormous desk in front of an entire wall of windows.

Marshall barely looked outside as he rounded the desk and set his briefcase on it. But Esther felt drawn to them as if they were a powerful magnet. "Your plantation," she said, her voice full of awe.

The rows and rows of pineapple plants were neat and orderly. Pathways had obviously been perfectly spaced to

allow tractors to spray fertilizer, ethylene, and other prod-
ucts onto them. The plants closest to the building, just on the
other side of a drainage ditch, each had a bright green
pineapple growing from the center.

"One fruit per plant," she said. "It's incredible."

He joined her, close enough to say they were together,
but without touching her. "They are pretty, aren't they?"

"I mean, I've toured your southern plantation, but not for
years. It was one of the first things we did as a family when
we moved here." Esther wanted to reach out and touch the
sweet fruit the way she had as a fourteen-year-old. She could
smell the sticky-sweet juice on the plantation and the rich,
fertile soil. "My brother would've loved it."

His arm came around her then, and Esther leaned into
him for comfort. "You miss him?" he asked.

"Every now and then," she said. "He was only seventeen
when he died, and I was the annoying little sister, you know?"

Marshall didn't nod or laugh, so Esther didn't either.
"George and I are close now."

"I'd like to meet your family." Marshall's hot breath
touched her ear, floated down her neck, and Esther shivered.
She couldn't imagine bringing him to George's wing house.
Marshall was far too refined for corn nuts and karaoke. And
bad karaoke at that.

But she smiled up at him and said, "Let's do the cake,"
with as much enthusiasm as she could.

He groaned, but it had a good-natured edge to it, and he
sat down when she pointed to his chair. She got out the
candles and made a big show of putting them on the cake

she'd baked herself. All she could do while she tried to get the lighter going was hope that the cake wasn't disgusting. She wasn't exactly known for her prowess in the kitchen.

With slightly trembling fingers, she tried the lighter again. Marshall's long, slender fingers closed over hers, steadying her and strengthening her. Her eyes drifted to his, and their gazes locked. She imagined herself growing old with him, watching as his dark hair turned gray, getting to come to these plantations and learn the pineapple business for herself.

She shook her head and looked down. Marshall pressed the ignitor, and the flame burst out of the end of the lighter. He directed her hands to light the candles, and then his touch fell away.

Esther hesitated for another moment, her thoughts still revolving around her car service. She wouldn't be giving that up in favor of pineapples, even if she and Marshall did get married.

*Focus*, she told herself. It hadn't even been a week yet, and her fantasies had already started taking on a white-dress, long-aisle theme.

"Happy birthday," she sang. He laughed then, but she pressed on, completing the song and saying, "Blow 'em out, you big, brawny billionaire."

His face radiated pure joy as he leaned forward and blew out his birthday candles. Esther stood back and watched him, basking in his beauty, his kind spirit, his goodness, until he looked at her.

"So you actually eat cake, right?" She flew into the next

phase of this party by collecting the plates, forks, and napkins she'd brought from her bag.

"I ran an extra two miles this morning." He puffed out his flat stomach. "So cake me. A big piece."

She couldn't remember a time when she'd felt so happy, so content, as she did cutting a chocolate birthday cake in his office. They talked about nonessential things as they each ate their piece, and Esther hoped she'd be around for his thirty-ninth birthday celebration too.

Soon enough, though, his phone rang and he swiped open the call with, "Hey, Fish."

Esther tried not to look like she was eavesdropping on the conversation, and since she actually had quite a bit of experience listening without looking like she was, she was able to hear his side of the conversation.

Several words caught in her ears. Words she'd heard before, and she'd always wondered at them. When Marshall hung up, she decided to be brave.

"So I've heard you mention something about Hawaii Nine-0 several times," she said. "You just did again. What is that?"

He blinked at her, and Esther mentally kicked herself. "Oh, it's a secret."

"It's not a secret." He sounded a little rehearsed. A titch mechanical.

"You look like I've hit you with a frying pan."

"It's…elite."

"Code word for secret." She rolled her eyes. "I get it. You and *Fish* have your own little club and I'm not invited." Well, she had a club too, thank you very much. And

Marshall *definitely* wasn't invited to sit on the beach with all the women who'd sworn off men. Or maybe that wasn't what the Women's Beach Club was at all. Esther had lost track over the course of the past week and a half, and she didn't like the loss of control.

Marshall leaned back in his chair, his power suit and his steepled fingers making him very much the untouchable billionaire he was. Who he'd always been.

"All right," he said, a smile playing across his mouth. "So I have a little club. It's nothing special, and it's exclusive, and maybe I don't want to hurt your feelings."

"What's the requirement to join?" Not that she really wanted to join. She had to have some spheres of her life that were Marshall-free. Didn't she?

"You have to have nine zeroes in your bank account. The Nine-Zero club. Not nine-oh."

Esther rummaged around in her bag like the extra zero she needed would be inside. "Oh. Well."

"And you have to live in Hawaii."

"Which I obviously do." She gave him a somewhat scathing look that fell short of burning him. "I'm not quite there yet."

"You'll get there."

She appreciated his confidence. "How many members are in your little club?"

"Nine."

"Ah, a good ol' boys club."

"Not at all. There are two women."

Great. Just what she needed. Handsome, charming, smart Marshall hanging out with two women with just as much money as him. A rush of jealousy moved through her, and not only because of the numbers in the bank account.

"It's no big deal," he said, going back to his paperwork. "We get together and talk business. You don't even like to talk business."

"Sure I do," she said. "I just don't want someone who knows nothing about my business to give me unsolicited advice." She nodded once at him and lifted her eyebrows as if to punctate the statement with *So there.*

He chuckled and held up the hand not holding a pen in surrender. "I get it, Esther. I was wrong to do that. Won't happen again."

"Unless I ask you."

He gazed at her evenly, the spark that had sprung to life last Sunday present, and hot, and getting hotter. "Unless you ask me."

She really did pull out the work she needed to accomplish that day, giving a little sniff like everything was settled.

He chuckled again. "When you get to be a billionaire yourself, we'll pull your financial records, and if everything checks out, I'll personally introduce you to the group."

"Thank you," she murmured, wondering if she could even handle another club, especially one where she had to prove actual worth to join.

———

## JOIN ELANA'S LIST

She arrived on the beach several hours later, having left Marshall's office just after they'd finished eating—kalua pork and sticky rice, from her favorite Hawaiian hut on Main Street, PolyFusion—without telling him about her own club meeting.

To be fair, Tawny had texted five minutes before lunch with *WBC two-thirty. Met a man.*

Esther had tried texting her for the details, but Tawny was keeping her thumbs off the keyboard. Probably because she wanted a bigger audience for news like this.

No matter what, Esther promised Marshall she'd be back by five-thirty, and she'd gone home to change, breathe in some soothing peppermint to quell the rolling in her stomach, and grab her beach bag.

When she approached the group of women already sitting on the outer edge of Sweet Breeze's private beachfront, she told herself over and over to keep her news to herself. She hadn't even told Stacey about the mind-blowing kiss with Marshall, and she didn't want to overshadow Tawny.

"Hey, girls." She sighed as she kicked off her flip flops and laid out her towel. A lot of the other women brought beach chairs so they could sit up, but Esther didn't mind sitting directly on the sand. She felt more connected to the island that way, and she'd always come to the beach when she needed that grounding.

A chorus of hellos and heys met her ears, and she scanned the group for Stacey. She hadn't arrived yet. Esther felt quite sure that Tawny wouldn't spill anything about a new man until their unofficial leader was there.

Sure enough, when Winnie Broadhead, the owner of Hibiscus Ink, a popular tattoo and piercing parlor on the island, asked, "So? Come on, Tawny. The suspense is killing me," Tawny frowned.

"It is not," she said. "You don't even want to be in another relationship." She took a long drink from her mug, and Esther found it strange it wasn't her usual soda.

"No, I don't," Winne said without shame or embarrass-ment. "But that doesn't mean I don't want you to be happy. And you do want to find someone and fall in love. So tell us what happened."

Tawny glanced down the beach, where it curved and the jungle clawed it's way toward the sand, only held back by a four-foot high stone wall. Aloha Hideaway, Stacey's bed and breakfast, sat back in the trees somewhere, with the most charming gardens.

Even Esther had dreamt about what it would be like to walk down the cobbled path, a long, white train behind her, as she approached the man she was in love with. And Tawny? Tawny probably had a date booked already.

"I haven't heard from her," Esther said quietly, hoping only Tawny could hear.

She gave herself a little shake, a look of doubt crossing

her face. Esther put her hand on Tawny's arm. "We'll fill her in, Tawny. Tell us."

She drew in a big breath, expanding her chest fully before blowing it out. "Okay, I met a man on the beach today. I've seen him before, actually. But he always looks like he's asleep. Today he was throwing a Frisbee to his dog and it flew into my class."

Esther watched the other women in the group, and they all seemed rapt as Tawny told her tale. Esther was too, if she were being perfectly honest with herself. Meeting a good-looking man for the first time was pulse-pounding and she didn't want to miss a word of the story.

And maybe, just maybe, her Women's Beach Club, which Esther had always thought would stick together forever, would be changing very soon. Did that mean she couldn't come to this patch of sand and talk with her friends?

*Of course not*, her mind whispered, and a wisp of the worry she'd felt about telling them about Marshall evaporated under the hot sun.

"Anyway," Tawny said, and Esther realized she'd missed some of the story. "He said he doesn't have a job, and that sent up a red flag. I mean, I don't want a man who doesn't work." She glanced around at the other ladies. "Do I?"

"What's his name?" Winnie asked. She knew a lot of people on the island, having grown up here. Her family was generational Hawaiians, and she leaned a bit closer to Tawny.

"Tyler. I didn't get a last name."

"Oh, I know him," Sasha said. "Surfer dude, longish blond hair?"

"Yeah, that's him," Tawny said.

"His last name is Rigby." Sasha reached for her phone. "And honey, he's *riiiich*. He doesn't need to work because he's already a billionaire." She tapped and typed, finally turning the phone toward Tawny, and then flashing it around the group.

"He won millions playing poker, then started the biggest online gambling website in the world." Sasha looked back at the phone, her dark eyes devouring whatever was on the screen. "Says here he sold his half of the company to his brother, the co-founder, for six-point-two billion dollars."

Esther immediately knew he was in the Hawaii Nine-0 club with Marshall, but she kept her lips tightly shut. He hadn't specifically asked her not to say anything, but she knew instinctively that she shouldn't.

"So are you going out with him?" Winnie asked.

"Still working toward the ask," Tawny said. "But Esther has a new beau."

All eyes lasered in on Esther, whose heart started sprinting like it would win a gold medal if it raced fast enough.

"Tawny."

"Come on," she said, scooting down in her chair and extending her legs. "We need to hear a hopeful story. Have you kissed him yet?"

Esther looked around the group, the eager glints she saw in each eye a testimony that while they were here, they still hadn't given up on love. And Esther realized she hadn't either.

"What's his name?" Sasha asked.

"It's the guy who owns all the pineapple plantations," Tawny said before Esther could respond.

"How about you tell it?" Esther reached into her bag for the bar of chocolate she'd brought.

"Sorry, sorry." Tawny flashed her a smile. "But do go on. I'm dying to know how the date on Thursday night went."

**WANT TO FIND OUT IF TAWNY GETS HER DATE WITH THE BILLIONAIRE BEACH BUM? READ THE BASHFUL BILLIONAIRE NOW!**

# TWELVE

MARSHALL WISHED Fisher hadn't given up alcohol, as he could really use a drink tonight. A couple of weeks had passed, and he liked Esther as much today as he had the day she'd laid a blue-wrapped package on the back seat.

More, in fact. He couldn't keep his hands to himself whenever he saw her, and every evening ended with her wrapped in his arms, their kisses as sweet as they were sexy.

Fisher had left a couple of days ago to go help his mother, who had suffered a couple of broken bones in a car accident. And Marshall had just gotten off the phone with Esther. A call that had started with accusations about his best friend, as if she were Stacey's personal bodyguard.

He raked his hands through his hair and paced in Fisher's suite. He had a call out to Fisher too, but he honestly didn't know how this was any of his problem. Stacey had freaked out about Fish leaving town, but Marshall would've done the same for his mother.

He passed the empty liquor cabinet, glad for its bare shelves now. He didn't like the way alcohol clouded his thinking, and he needed to get his thoughts straight as an arrow.

Because his mother had asked him about Esther. How she'd found out, Marshall wasn't entirely sure. He hadn't deliberately kept the relationship a secret, but he hadn't brought her to any of the Thursday dinners in the few short weeks they'd been dating, and she hadn't asked to come.

The door opened, and he turned to find Tyler, Lawrence, and Ira entering the room. Tyler wore a pair of board shorts and a T-shirt with triangle on it. He was the least likely to be labeled a billionaire, but Marshall knew better. Beneath all those surfer locks and devil-may-care attitude, the man managed his money like he only had pennies left.

Lawrence and Ira fit the mold of the Nine-0 club, and they were already talking about the new tariffs on consumable exports. Marshall suddenly didn't want to talk business, and he decided he wouldn't. Such talk wasn't a requirement at the meeting, and he handed Tyler a can of soda with a nod.

"How's the beach?"

"Fantastic." He grinned and popped the top. "How are the pineapples?"

"Fantastic." The plantations had made a full recovery from the storm, and Marshall had new plants in the ground and fruit being harvested and shipped every day.

His phone rang, and a rush of relief filled him at Fisher's impeccable timing. "It's Fish," he said, already putting long strides between him and the other members of the club. The bell rang again, signaling that another elevator full of people had arrived.

Marshall ducked into the guest room off the living room and answered the call. "Fish."

"Hey, Marshall. How are things on the islands?"

"There aren't any storms," he said.

"Well, that's good."

"Yeah."

"Look, I need to ask you something."

"Shoot."

"Have you talked to Esther or anything?" Fisher sounded frustrated.

Yeah, he talked to Esther about a lot of things. The men that claimed her shallow or that they didn't know her obviously hadn't tried that hard. "About what, exactly?"

"Stacey."

Marshall's pulse blipped. "Why would I talk to her about Stacey?"

"Apparently she thinks I left her."

"Did you?"

Fisher hissed into the phone. "My mother was in a car accident. I'm in Michigan. Temporarily."

"But you did leave without telling her." Marshall didn't mean to sound like such a jerk. He understood business and family, but knew very little about women and relationships. Obviously, Fisher operated by the same manual.

"I asked Owen to send her a message, and she never got it." Fisher sounded tired, and Marshall imagined him rubbing his eyes as he spoke.

"Esther said she's not in a good place," he said. "Maybe give Stacey some time."

"Yeah."

Marshall wanted to end the call, but he decided he could ask a question of his own. "So...what do you think of inviting an almost-billionaire to the Nine-0 club?"

"What?"

That was all Marshall needed to know. "Never mind. It's a stupid idea."

"Who is it?"

He didn't want to say, but he pushed out, "Esther," anyway. "She doesn't qualify, but I'm...I'm actually thinking of buying Your Ride for over a billion dollars. Then she would."

"Wow. I—" Fisher didn't say anything for a few seconds, and Marshall's idea sounded ridiculous and stupid when he said it out loud. What made him think Esther would even sell to him? So she could come to Fish's swanky twenty-eighth floor suite and sip water while boring business people talked about taxes and investments?

This club wasn't even her scene, and yet he felt guilty for being here without her. She hadn't asked what his "meeting" was but the woman was as sharp as a tack. She had to know.

"How do you know she's even a millionaire?" Fish asked.

"I looked her up."

"You mean you pulled strings and looked at her private financials."

"Something like that."

"Why would you do that?"

"I can't believe you don't," Marshall hadn't had this argument in a long time. But Fish had never been married, though he had told Marshall about a woman who'd tried to get him drunk and then to sign over a huge chunk of his assets. So he should understand, at least a little. But he didn't seem to.

"She isn't going to like that," Fish said.

"She isn't going to find out." But Marshall had this nagging feeling in the back of his mind that he needed to be honest with her. Hadn't he already told her that he hoped they'd always be truthful with each other?

"She's not going to sell Your Ride," Fish said. "She built that place from nothing."

Marshall nodded, though his best friend was a world away. "You're right. I don't know why I'm even thinking about it."

"I don't either. Besides, what would you do with a car service?"

"Let her run it."

"So this is just about getting her the zeroes she needs."

Marshall ran his hand down his face, the beard he hadn't shaved for a couple of days starting to itch. "I don't know."

"Oh, I get it now." Fisher started laughing, and that only made Marshall angry on top of confused.

"Get what?"

"You're falling in love with her."

"No," Marshall said automatically. *No.*

"You are," Fish insisted. "And you're trying to make sure she's on the up and up, that's why you pulled her financials. To make sure she's not after your money." So Fisher knew too much of Marshall's background. Didn't mean he was right.

"And you don't want the Nine-0 club to come between you, so you're trying to figure out a way for her to join."

"No," Marshall said again, but everything Fisher had said was starting to sound true. "Tyler's calling me. Tell your mother I hope she feels better from me."

Fisher laughed, and Marshall hung up with the sound of it ringing in his ears. He didn't go back out to the living room and the meeting though. He couldn't believe he'd allowed himself to slip down the slippery love slope so dang fast.

Three weeks. Fine, three and a half. It had only taken him three and a half weeks to start thinking about having Esther in his life permanently.

And he had no idea what to do with her.

He did know she had money of her own, and her interest in him seemed to be one-hundred percent genuine. He knew he was happier with her by his side, even when they weren't talking, than he was alone. He knew she kissed him with as much fervor as he kissed her.

"But are you in love with her?" he asked.

He couldn't answer the question, and when Tyler did poke his head into the room, Marshall left the unanswered thought in the guest suite and went back to the meeting, where such perplexities didn't exist.

————

Marshall strolled down the sand, his hand secure in Esther's. Another week had gone by, and he wasn't exactly sure what he'd done at work. But he knew he'd shown Esther around his house, and she hadn't judged him for the massive theater room he'd only used twice. They'd eaten sashimi, which she'd brought over with her, and watched the sun sink into the ocean.

He'd never pegged himself for a romantic guy, but Esther seemed to think he was topping the charts.

She cooked dinner for him at her bungalow, but everything had been too salty. "Ew, gross. Don't eat that." She'd practically lunged at him to get the plate with chicken and rice away, and then they'd gone down the beach to a hut that sold wraps with everything imaginable in them.

They'd wandered through the jungle trees on the way back, and he felt like he'd gotten lost in the forest with her—which was just fine by him. His world had narrowed with her in it, and he liked it.

She'd stopped opening the door for him, and he'd kept paying the same amount. He wasn't going to bring it up again, not if she didn't. They swam in Fisher's private pool, as he was still in Michigan with his mom. Stacey had gone too, and all seemed to be well with them.

By the end of the week, Marshall had the growing need to let Esther know how he was feeling. Cards, flowers, dinner dates, sailing, chocolates, he'd done them all.

Esther was fond of coffee, and essential oils, and the beach.

Truth be told, Marshall had started thinking in terms of diamonds and how he could surprise the woman that seemed to know everything about his life before he did. She knew a lot of his favorite things, and he'd enjoyed learning about lavender oil to help him sleep and peppermint oil for when his stomach hurt. Not that he'd ever use them, but he found it sweet that Esther subscribed to the health benefits of oils, and he knew the money in that industry was *huge*.

But he didn't want to get her a new stock of jasmine oil. He needed to know a few more things about her before he took the next step, because the next step had his feet on glass ground, and it could shatter at any moment.

"So," he said on Friday evening when they'd cuddled together in the hammock she had hanging on the edge of her property. She'd confessed and told him she only owned one of the trees, but so far, no one from the forest service had come complaining about her use of the second one.

"So," she repeated when he let his train of thought keep going without saying anything.

He liked the soft vanilla scent of her hair, the feel of her body formed to his. Getting his next words out was so, so hard. He cleared his throat, the sliver of sky he could see through the foliage above the bluest he'd ever seen. It darkened toward navy, giving him the courage he needed. After all, Esther had told him a few days ago that his navy suits were her favorite.

"I'm just going to say this," he said.

"That would be great," she teased.

He should've relaxed, but he wasn't sure if they were this far along in their relationship or not. He just knew he wanted to be.

"So in the Robison family, the first born takes over all

operations of the plantations at age thirty," he started, unsure of why he thought she needed a family history lesson. "So I've been doing that for a few years. But at age forty, the plantations become mine. My father will be retired, and I'll pay him a salary."

"Okay," she said. "Sounds great."

"I don't have a first born," he said.

"Ah, and you're wondering if I want kids."

"Do you?"

Esther remained silent, and Marshall pushed the hammock slightly with his free hand, giving her time to think, absorb, and respond. It was a skill he'd learned from her over the past couple of months, and though the silence made his pulse do weird skippy things, he kept his mouth shut.

"I'd like children," she finally said.

Pure relief soared through him, and he took a deep breath of her, inhaling the essence of her all the way to the bottom of his heart. "I think I'm in love with you."

Marshall hadn't said words like that in so, so long, and it felt amazing. Another freeing moment when he hadn't even realized he'd been caged.

Esther twisted to look at him, her eyes brimming with tears. "Are you serious?"

"Deadly."

She closed her eyes, and a single track of tears ran down her left cheek. He wiped it with his free hand and guided her mouth to his. This kiss was different than any of the previous. There was no rush, but still plenty of passion. The love flowing between them was palpable, almost hanging in the air with the humidity.

And Esther hadn't said *I love you* back, but she didn't need to. Marshall could feel it in her kiss, and that was good enough for now.

"I'm not crazy, am I?" he asked, pushing her hair back from her face and gazing down at her.

She pressed her lips together and shook her head, her eyes still closed. "I've loved you for years," she whispered, and his heart catapulted around inside his chest. "I was worried you might not live up to the man in my dreams, but you have."

She opened her eyes and said again, "You have."

Marshall smiled a gooey smile at her, one that felt stretched and soft like a warmed marshmallow. "I hope I can always be the man of your dreams."

And he really did, but something scratched at the back of his mind, reminding him that he still had some secrets to tell her.

*Later*, he thought as she kissed him again. For now, this moment was perfect, and this moment was all that mattered.

# THIRTEEN

ESTHER SQUINTED down at her phone, sure it hadn't just gone off. But it had, and the clock on the lock screen read 4:45. Didn't her dad know she got up at five o'clock as it was? She couldn't have her fifteen minutes of beauty sleep?

She sighed and lifted the phone above her head, still trying to get her eyes to adjust to the bright screen. His message read *Come by before work today if you can. Have something I want to talk to you about.*

It was Saturday, and Stacey was in Michigan, making her relationship with Fisher right, and Esther honestly didn't know what was on the schedule for today. Jaylani took care of things, and she'd been focusing on Marshall more and more, especially since he'd said he loved her.

She let her phone rest on her chest, her smile the only thing she could hold up right now. Marshall Robison loved her. She wasn't sure what world she'd been transported to, but she wanted to stay forever.

Eventually, she got up and went through her morning routine. When she arrived at her parent's house, she didn't go inside. Her father would be in the shed, prepping the fruit for the farmer's market, which started at nine o'clock. At barely seven, they should have plenty of time to talk.

"Dad." She found him wiping down the skin of a papaya.

"Esther, there you are." He abandoned the fruit, an anxious look on his face that made Esther feel like a terrible accident had happened.

"Where's Mom?" she asked. "Is she okay?"

His eyebrows drew down and he said, "Your mom is fine. I have—I—" His fingers wound around and around each other, and Esther didn't understand why he was so nervous.

"Dad." She drew the word out, a clear warning for him to spit it out already.

"So I have an alert on each of us," he said carefully. "Me, your mother, George, and you, and something came up in your monthly summary."

Esther had no idea what her father was talking about. "Dad, you've got to explain to me like I'm three."

"So I monitor financial information, right? Prevent fraud, develop systems to keep personal information behind strong firewalls."

"Yeah, sure," Esther said. She knew her*f* father was in the financial security field, and she knew he could track credit card numbers. She'd asked him to do it for Fisher, and that was how she and Stacey had learned he'd left the island in the middle of the night.

What she didn't know was her role in anything.

"So I have an alert on us," he said. "If someone runs our numbers, a credit card, pulls our credit report, that kind of thing."

Esther nodded, her muscles tightening. She folded her arms across her stomach, desperate for something to eat though she rarely ate breakfast.

"Someone looked at all of your information," he said, his face grave. "Your personal accounts, and your business profile."

The words sounded like English, but Esther didn't quite know what they meant. "How do you know?"

"It came on your monthly summary, like I said. The bank shows a financial check on June twenty-third. Did you do that?"

She didn't even know what a financial check was. When she told her father that, he shook his head and ground his teeth together. "That makes no sense. Who would want to see your wealth?" He paced back toward the crates of fruit. He spun back to her. "You haven't noticed anything suspicious, have you? Charges you don't recognize?"

"No, all of my accounts are fine." Esther had given some responsibility to Jaylani, but the woman had kept excellent receipts and records, and everything in the accounts was accurate and up-to-date. Esther did most of the bookkeeping herself, so she knew.

Her dad picked up the cloth he'd been using on the papayas. "Well, someone looked at them. Your credit. Your debt to income ratio. All of it. They know how much money you have, and what outstanding balances and which places."

Esther sank onto an empty apple crate. "Why would someone need to know that?" Her mind raced, revolving around the sensitive information in her bank accounts. "Do I need to close my accounts and get new ones?"

"It happened weeks ago," her father said. "If you haven't noticed anything awry, then you're probably fine. I'd keep an eye on it. Could your weekend manager have done this?"

Jaylani had barely known how to put the receipts in the financial software Esther used. There was no way she'd know how to pull financial records like the kind her father was talking about.

The answer hit her like a bolt of lightning.

No, Jaylani couldn't do something like that. But Marshall totally could.

*Marshall.*

The whip of betrayal stung her heart, and a moan actually leaked from her mouth. "I have to go, Dad." She kept her focus on her phone so her father wouldn't be able to see the agony as it ripped through her chest.

"Esther," her dad called after her, but Esther kept her feet moving. Once in the safety of her car, with the doors locked as if someone would happen by and demand to see all the conversations on her phone, she tapped out a message to Marshall.

*We need to talk.*

———

Esther drummed her thumbs on the steering wheel as she drove the winding roads toward Marshall's cliffside manor. He hadn't seemed alarmed by her ominous text, but she couldn't get her stomach to stop shaking. A confrontation with a client was so far out of her routine that she felt like the earth would crack and swallow her whole.

"This is not a client visit," she told herself for the third time. "He's your boyfriend, and you guys were just talking about having a family together last night."

As if on cue, her guts twisted. Oh, how she wanted a baby. As the years had passed and she'd settled into her career and her friends, she'd shelved the idea of being a mother. But there Marshall had been, bringing it up and adding a new layer to her fantasies with him.

"You don't even know if it was him," she said to the silence in the car.

"But who else could it have been?" she argued back.

She shook her head, willing herself to stop talking to herself. She'd just go see him, ask him, and find out the truth.

Fear gripped her pulse, making it stop for a moment. Maybe she didn't need the truth. But Marshall had said they could be honest with each other.

Her thoughts continued to be as twisted as the roads, until she finally arrived at his gate. She knew the code, and yet she couldn't bring herself to tap it into the keypad. She'd been here thousands of times, the nose of the car almost touching the metal in front of her.

She pressed her eyes closed and tried to think. There had been no time to discuss the situation with Stacey or any of the other girls. Maybe she should stall. Text Marshall and tell him another job came up and get back to the beach as fast as possible.

Or maybe she could solve her own problems. After all, she knew in her heart of hearts that the Beach Club wouldn't last forever.

"Just do it," she said. She pressed a bit too hard on the button to get the window to roll down, and she may have jabbed at the numbers in the code.

The gate rumbled open, and she eased the car onto his property. She parked, and got out, and faced the double front doors like they were the mouth of the monster and she was going to willingly step through.

Marshall opened the door before she could take a single step. His tall frame filled the new space, and he was the sexiest man she'd ever laid eyes on. He looked fresh from the gym, wearing athletic shorts and a T-shirt that was way too small for his broad chest and shoulders.

He didn't smile, the first indication that he'd heard the underlying message in her text.

Esther fisted her fingers and moved up the steps. Marshall didn't budge from the doorway, didn't fall back so she could go inside. The breeze up here was more of a wind, catching Esther's hair and pulling on it.

"I need to ask you a question," she said.

"All right." He moved then, walking back into the foyer of his house and sitting on the third step of the freestanding staircase.

Esther had enjoyed the home tour she'd gotten a week or so ago. His house was beautiful, but it had a functional feel, almost like he didn't really live here. But she'd still enjoyed the big spaces, the high-end finishes, the special details that made the house stand out. Her entire bungalow could fit inside the foyer, and while she had plenty of money to upgrade to a house as fancy as this one, she had no idea what she'd fill it with.

*Empty.*

That was how his house felt. How her heart felt.

She looked right at Marshall, not wanting to miss a single flick of his eyes. "Someone looked into my finances several weeks ago. My personal finances and my business finances, almost like they were checking for something." She paused, waited, watched.

He simply looked at her, blinking at a normal rate. Her heart beat settled and then picked up again as she prepared to speak.

"Was it you?" she asked.

"Yes."

No hesitation. No apology. No emotion. She'd seen him wall off his emotions before, during business calls, while riding in the back seat long before they'd started dating, when his mother called.

But never with her.

"Why?"

"Honestly? I was covering my bases. I check into everyone I do business with."

*Do business with.*

The words stabbed Esther right in the softest part of her heart. She didn't like this version of Marshall Robison, and it was the first time she'd ever thought that.

As the air leaked from her lungs like a punctured tire, she drew herself up. She would not show him that he'd hurt her. Not now. Not ever.

She gestured between them. "This." She took a moment to steady her voice. "*This* is not business."

She wished with everything in her that she'd put on her power suit and heels that morning. Because turning on her sandaled toe and marching out of his house didn't have the same effect as it would've otherwise.

He called after her, but she didn't turn back. The door slammed closed behind her, and her chest heaved as she ran to the car. Behind the wheel, a sense of belonging filled her. This was where she belonged. Behind the wheel of this car.

Not in Marshall's house. Not in his arms. Or his life.

A sob worked its way up her throat, but she choked it back, glancing to the front steps as she put the car in drive and practically stomped on the accelerator.

Marshall stood there, his hands hanging limply at his sides, a hard look on his face.

Esther might have gone back had he looked like he cared that she was about to drive out of his life. But he didn't, and she did exactly that.

# FOURTEEN

MARSHALL STOOD on the steps for a long time. Long after the sound of Esther's engine died. Long after the sun had started to heat the stones. Long after he should've gone back inside to call Esther and explain everything.

Why had he said their relationship was business?

*Idiot*, he chastised himself when he finally got up enough brainpower to move back into the house. It felt cavernous, like it would smother him if he stayed too long.

He showered, dressed, and called a cab. No, he didn't have a car. But he could still get around the island if he had to.

"Sweet Breeze," he said to the driver when he arrived. The ride down the mountain in a car that smelled like grease and sweat wasn't nearly as fun as driving with Esther. He had a feeling nothing would be as fun without her.

*Why* had he said that?

Why hadn't he told her earlier?

Why had he checked into her financials in the first place?

Too many why's, and Marshall couldn't answer any of them anyway.

At Sweet Breeze, he'd just collapsed on Fisher's couch when the man called him. "Yeah?" Marshall sounded miserable, even to his own ears.

He wasn't sure he'd ever felt like this before. Hollowed out. No hope. Wanting to just fall asleep until the pain and hurt and washed out feeling of losing Esther had dissipated.

Because he knew it would. He'd been devastated when he'd discovered Lorna's behind-the-scenes activities. But he'd been fueled by anger then. By betrayal and bitterness.

Now he had nothing. Nothing but his own flaws to blame for pushing away the woman he loved.

"Hey," Fish said, his voice on the outer edge of excitement. "I have a favor to ask you."

"Anything." At least it would give Marshall something to focus on. Something to do. A purpose for his life. Just last night he'd thought he might actually be able to keep the pineapple plantations in his family, because he'd *have* a family. Everything had changed with one text and a five-minute conversation.

"So I'm going to ask Stacey to marry me when I get back to the island," Fish said, his words practically tripping over themselves. "And I want it to be a big surprise, and I need your help to pull it off."

Marshall felt like Fisher had jumped on his chest with the words *marry me*. A slow hiss came out of his mouth, but he said, "Yeah, sure, whatever you need." His voice wavered, but Fish was obviously too excited to notice.

"I've already talked to Owen, and I have room fifteen-twenty-one booked. I'm going to overnight a ring to you. I need it in the room, on the armoire. And I'm going to text you a number. That's Tayla over at Aloha Hideaway. She's going to sneak you into Stacey's gardens, where she has the only blue-purple hibiscus flowers available. Her grandfather cultivated them, and she loves them. I want vases of them in room fifteen-twenty-one."

Marshall squeezed his eyes shut and rubbed two fingers along his forehead. "When does this need to be done?"

"I'm coming back in three days."

"Three days." He should be able to get some flowers in a vase in three days. "You got it."

"I'm coming in on the eleven-ten flight. Stacey and I will go to lunch, and then I've got a meeting."

"Oh?"

"The meeting is fake," he said. "I need the room ready by noon, Tuesday."

"Noon, Tuesday," Marshall repeated, his heart only a shell now. His best friend sounded so happy. Full of joy. And Marshall wanted that for himself—he'd had it yesterday. Memories of last night in the hammock paraded through his mind, a cruel reminder of what he'd had. What he'd ruined by his inability to trust.

He hung up with Fisher, one thought running through his brain: *How do I fix this?*

---

Nothing came while he shopped for the best vases Getaway Bay offered. He found one in Fisher's own gift shop, a beautiful, blue glass vase that stood almost two feet tall. He took it to the appointed room on the fifteenth floor and headed out again.

He walked down the street, mourning the loss of his ride. He'd spend the next few days away from the office, so he wouldn't have to bother Esther. As he approached Your Ride, he decided to go in and cancel his service until Wednesday morning. Then Fish would be back, and Marshall could buy some time until he figured out how to get past his issues and get Esther back into his life.

After all, Stacey had done that. She'd been so mad at Fisher for leaving in the middle of the night. Even if his reason was good, it had triggered everything Stacey feared. But she'd gotten on a plane and gone to Michigan and made things right.

He glanced around the office space, but he didn't see Esther. Not that he expected to. She had a weekend manager, and the only job she did on Saturdays and Sundays was drive him.

A Hawaiian woman wearing a black dress and a bright blue lei greeted him. "Good morning. I'm Jaylani. How can I help you, Mister Robison?"

"I'm not going to be going into the office for a few days." He rapped his knuckles on the counter in front of him. "Can you let Esther know she doesn't need to come until Wednesday morning?"

Jaylani wrote a couple of words on a sticky pad in front of her. "Same time Wednesday?"

"Yes, please."

The woman beamed at him. "I'll let her know." If she found it strange he couldn't just text the same request to Esther, Jaylani didn't make it known. He cast one final glance around the place before turning to go.

He managed to find another vase at a glass-blowing shop across from the worst sushi restaurant on the island. For the lunch crowd, the line spilled out the door, and Marshall shook his head at it.

*What?* he heard in Esther's coy, flirtatious voice. *Their sushi isn't up to your standards?*

At which point, she'd laugh, toss that beautiful head of hair over her shoulder, and look at him with stars in her eyes.

And no, their sushi was *not* up to his standards. He looked east, in the direction of Esther's bungalow. She lived about a mile from her office, so he couldn't actually see her house. But he knew what it felt like to be there, with her. He knew that it smelled like lavender and lilacs, and flowers and fragrances that belonged only to her.

He knew he wanted to go there.

He turned away and walked back the way he'd come. He still needed one more vase, but he had two and a half more days to procure the necessary items. He didn't want to be so close to Esther's office, or her house, or the roads she drove. If he saw her, he wasn't sure what would happen. If she was behind the wheel of a car, he wouldn't put it past her to run him down.

And he deserved it.

He went back to Sweet Breeze and found Fisher's head

valet talking to another employee. He motioned for Sterling to come speak with him when he was finished, and a few minutes later, he asked, "Can I take Fish's car for a couple of days? He has some things he wants me to do for him."

If Sterling could see the slight fib in those words, he didn't indicate as much. Marshall felt like half of himself, because in the past he probably would've just told Sterling to bring him the car. He wouldn't have *asked*.

"Let me call Mister DuPont," Sterling said. He stepped away, ever the dutiful employee, and made the call. Five minutes later, Marshall had the keys as well as a text from Fish that said, *Esther's not driving you anymore? What happened?*

Suddenly dedicated to not driving while texting, Marshall tossed his phone to the passenger seat and put both hands on the wheel. But he had no destination he wanted to go to.

So he just drove.

———

He woke to the sound of a jangling collar. He barely had time to throw his hands in front of his face before a golden retriever licked his face. "Ah," he groaned at the same time Tyler pulled the dog back.

"Lazy Bones," he chastised, but Marshall knew that was the retriever's name. "Leave 'im alone."

Why Tyler lived in a one-bedroom shack was beyond Marshall. The man had billions of dollars. Surely he could afford a second bedroom for guests.

Marshall sat up and wiped his face clean of dog slobber. "Going surfing?" he asked when he beheld Tyler in a rash guard and board shorts. Of course, the man wore something similar every day of his life, so he could've just as easily been going to the grocery store.

"Yeah. Killer waves on the north beach this morning."

Marshall exhaled and scrubbed his hands through his hair. "What time is it?"

"Five. Go back to sleep." But Tyler started banging around the kitchen, putting food together and making coffee. Marshall watched him, almost envious of the man's simple life. No job. No commitments, other than Lazy Bones, who sat very still at the end of the counter, waiting.

Tyler finally fed him and finished gathering the supplies he needed for that morning's waves. Despite growing up on the islands, Marshall had never gotten into surfing. He loved sailing, however, and he decided on the spot to take the catamaran out for the day. He could sleep on it if he took enough food. Maybe he wouldn't have to step foot back on land until his heart figured out how to beat instead of flop.

He probably should've gone to the boat last night. Or his own house. Or the one he owned on Maui. Or his parent's place. But nowhere had seemed safe from questions, safe from self-doubt. Tyler stayed up late and didn't ask questions, and he said, "Eat whatever you want. I'll be back later."

"I'll be gone." Marshall stood, intending to shower here, get some clothes and groceries, and head to the dock. "Thanks, man." He man-clapped Tyler on the back and shuffled toward the bathroom.

The door closed behind Tyler and Lazy Bones as Marshall looked at himself in the mirror. Yep. He definitely looked like a man who'd lost it all.

Again.

He turned away from his reflection, the thoughts from the previous night still floating around in his head.

He stewed on them while he showered, dressed, and drove up to his house. The emptiness of the place helped him find clarity of thought, and he dismissed the idea of calling Esther to see if she wanted to talk.

Of course she didn't. She probably knew by now that he'd canceled his service, otherwise she'd be showing up at his gate any minute. The thought sent panic through him, and he checked the screens in his bedroom to see if her car was waiting at the gate. Part of him hoped it was.

Nothing.

He packed quickly and stopped at the grocery store for convenience items he could eat without having to cook. The moment his foot touched the boat, relief spread through him.

Another text from Fish came in. *Are you ignoring me?*

*No.* Marshall sent the text and went back to the car for the rest of the groceries.

*You'll have everything ready?* he asked. *I thought you could work with Esther, but she says she has everything under control.*

*So do I.* Marshall thought the shorter his texts were, the sooner Fish would stop bothering him, the sooner he could get out on the water.

*Tayla's expecting to hear from you today.*

Marshall almost chucked his phone overboard. Instead he typed, *I know,* and set it to silent. He couldn't pick the hibiscus flowers today anyway. They'd look like trash by Tuesday.

No, right now he just needed to get out on the water and figure out how to live on this island with Esther and not have her in his life.

# FIFTEEN

ESTHER STAYED at Sweet Breeze on Saturday night, afraid that Marshall might come by her bungalow. Not in a stalker, creepy way, but an apologetic way. And she wanted to hold onto her anger for a little longer.

At least she hadn't been hacked by someone nefarious, who wanted to steal her assets from her. But Marshall didn't trust her, and she couldn't be with someone who would forever assume she would do the same thing his ex-wife had done.

Fisher's hotel was incredibly comfortable, and because Marshall had canceled his service for a few days, Esther had nowhere to be. Nothing to do. She'd been working nonstop for fifteen years, and it felt rewarding and relaxing to spend some extra time in bed, leafing through the room service menu.

She didn't quite feel like herself, and she suspected she might not for quite a while. After all, she'd given pieces of herself to Marshall, and she needed time to find them all and get them back.

*Beach this morning?* she texted to Tawny and Stacey, abandoning the idea of eating anything. *I broke up with Marshall.*

She'd managed to keep the news to herself for twenty-four hours, but now she needed reinforcements. Reassurance.

*Oh, honey,* Stacey's text came in. *Let me make sure Tayla can handle the checkouts, and I'll be right over.*

*I stayed at Sweet Breeze last night,* she messaged just as Tawny texted *I'll be there in ten.*

Esther didn't have any of her beach clothes. Her bag. Her lotions. Nothing.

She didn't care. She wasn't going to go get them. What if Marshall had slept in some work truck in her driveway? No, she had money and it was about time she spent some of it.

*Maybe thirty minutes, she said. I don't have any of my stuff and need to hit up Fisher's gift shop.*

She'd looked at exactly one bikini when Tawny stepped next to her. "Hey." She wrapped her skinny, muscular arms around Esther and held on tight. "I'm so sorry," she whispered.

Esther almost lost it right there in the Sweet Breeze gift shop. But she managed to pull in a breath tight enough to keep her emotions behind the wall.

"I'll get the sunglasses," Tawny said. She peered at Esther for an extra moment and then stepped over to the spinning stand, selecting the shiniest, mirrored shades from the rack.

Stacey arrived as Esther added a towel to her growing pile of purchases. She wore a worried look in her green eyes, and she too hugged Esther as if she'd just been diagnosed with a terrible, terminal disease.

Maybe she had. Maybe she'd never be able to find someone to spend her life with. A wave of hurt tore through her, and no amount of sucking at the air was going to hold back this emotion. She couldn't speak as the tears flowed down her face, and Stacey turned her toward the back of the store as she said, "Tawny."

She took everything from Esther and handed it to Tawny. She unshouldered Esther's purse and gave it to her too. "Go buy this stuff. Esther, come with me."

Esther let Stacey lead her out of the shop and around the corner, down a hall that obviously wasn't used by guests. Esther went, her lungs shaking, and her legs one step away from giving out. One more step. One more.

Stacey keyed in a code and the private elevator beeped. Less than a minute later, the car spat them out in a beautiful penthouse where Marshall had brought Esther previously—Fisher's residence.

Esther couldn't look at Stacey. If she did, she'd lose it.

"What happened?"

Esther shook her head and managed to get to the couch to sit. She covered her face with both hands and cried, something she'd never allowed herself to do with her previous boyfriends. Because Marshall was more than a boyfriend, and she knew it.

"I told him I loved him," she gasped out between the sobs. "We were talking about having a family."

Stacey joined her on the couch and wrapped both hands

around her shoulders, saying, "All right. Just let it out. Get it all out."

Esther leaned into her and sobbed, this heart break sharper than anything she'd ever experienced before.

———

They never did make it to the beach. Tawny showed up in the penthouse and they had their Beach Club meeting indoors for the first time as Esther cried herself dry and then told the whole story.

And Esther was very grateful for her friends. They were very good friends, and they didn't offer advice, or tell her what she should've done, or bash on Marshall. Somehow they knew that none of those things would really help. Just having them there was what Esther needed, and they all cuddled into the couch and put a romantic comedy on the television.

By the time the movie ended, Esther felt rusty, creaky, the lines on her face caked with salt from her tears. "Thank you," she said, pushing out a great big breath. "I better get to work."

"You don't work on the weekends," Stacey said.

"Well, I can't sit around here, feeling sorry for myself." Esther gave her friends a hug each, and they went down the elevator together.

Her office felt safe. Somewhere Marshall would never come. She pulled around the back of the building and sat in the car, wondering if she was being stupid. Neither Stacey nor Tawny had said so, but Esther couldn't help feeling foolish.

Deep down, she knew it wasn't embarrassment for how she'd acted at Marshall's yesterday. But humiliation that she'd told him she'd been in love with him for years, only to find out he had performed a background check on her and dug into her private and business finances.

*I check into everyone I do business with.*

The words hurt so much, and she wondered if they'd ever stop.

"Should've stuck to business," she muttered to herself. She turned off the car and went inside the building. She paused just inside the door, something new and different about the place. Jaylani sat at the counter, and she glanced up at Esther.

Surprise ran through her eyes. "Esther. What're you doing here?"

"I...." Esther didn't know how to explain. "I just wanted to get caught up on a few things for next week."

Jaylani stood, her expression radiating anxiety now. "I put something on your desk."

Esther approached slowly, like she might scare Jaylani off with too many quick movements. "What is it?"

"Someone stopped by today. He had something for you, but I told him you didn't work on the weekends. He said it was fine, that he didn't want to talk to you."

Esther raised her eyebrows. "He didn't want to talk to me, but he had something for me?" All kinds of alarms were going off in her head, and none of them were good. "Who was it?"

"I...can't say."

Esther narrowed her eyes, all her senses on overdrive now. "You can't? Or you don't know who it was?"

"I know who it was." Jaylani swallowed and ran her hand over her braided hair, a nervous gesture Esther hadn't seen from her in a long time. "He asked me not to tell you. I didn't think I'd have to, because I didn't think you'd be in until tomorrow, when you'd see the folder on your desk...." Her voice trailed into nothing and she glanced over her shoulder to Esther's office, where the door sat closed.

Esther cocked her head, in no mood for games. "Fine. I guess I'll go find out for myself." She half-expected Jaylani to step in front of her and stop her, but she just watched Esther walk by and enter her office.

She closed the door behind her, immediately spotting the blue folder on her desk, even amidst the other chaos she'd left on Friday. So maybe she kept a messy desk. Didn't mean she didn't know what every sheet of paper was, and where every report resided.

After rounding the desk, she gazed down at the folder as if she could see through the thick cardstock to the papers within. It wasn't thick, and she couldn't imagine what it would hold. She sat in her desk chair and opened the drawer. She had a bottle of frankincense there, and she dabbed a little behind each ear, inhaling the fragrant scent to help calm herself. Her oils had always worked for her, but she wasn't entirely sure even the best scents could ease this depression.

But she felt a bit calmer, and she opened the folder to find out what was inside. Her eyes couldn't read fast enough, but it didn't take long for her to understand the goal of the document. Someone wanted to buy Your Ride.

She flipped the page, searching for the buyer, and her blood ran cold when she saw Robison Enterprises.

She fell back in her chair as if the words had physically hit her. Marshall wanted to steal Your Ride from her?

Anger made her whole face hot, and she leaned forward again to find out how much he thought her business was worth. He ought to know; he'd pulled the financial records weeks ago.

Purchase price: $1,000,000,000

The air left Esther's lungs and leaked from her mouth in a low hiss.

"One billion dollars?" She slapped the folder closed and snatched it from the desk. Out in the front of the office, she said, "When did he drop this off?"

"A couple of hours ago." Jaylani stood, perceiving the storm that was about to hit the building. "Why? What is it?"

"A con," Esther said darkly. "Theft." She marched toward the door. "And if he comes back, call the cops."

"Mister Robison?"

"Yes. He's not welcome here." Esther knew Jaylani deserved more of an explanation, but she couldn't give it at the moment. Right now, she needed to talk to Marshall and find out what kind of sick game he was playing.

JOIN ELANA'S LIST

# SIXTEEN

MARSHALL WASN'T EXPECTING to see anyone for a few days, so when some very angry—and loud—knocking landed on his front door, he was both surprised and terrified. Only a handful of people knew the code to his gate, and he didn't want to see any of them right now.

He ran his hands through his hair as he walked over to the monitor that would show him the front porch.

"Esther." He breathed her name, more terrified than before, because she hugged the blue folder against her chest like a shield.

He twisted toward the door, wondering if he could simply not answer. He could claim almost anything. He'd been napping. Hadn't been home. It wasn't like he had a car and she'd know.

"Marshall!" she yelled. "You answer this door right now."

The sound of her voice, furious as it was, ignited

something inside him that had gone out when she'd broken up with him yesterday morning. The past thirty hours had been a special kind of torture, and he decided he'd rather have her yelling at him than not have her at all.

A spark started in him as he crossed to the front door and pulled it open. Esther's blue eyes danced with dangerous fire, and she slapped the folder against his chest as she moved right into his body.

"What is this?" she demanded. "Are you trying to steal my company?"

"*Steal* your company?" He scoffed and encircled her wrist with his fingers. "This is an offer, Esther. A very generous offer, in fact, for a thriving business."

"Your Ride is *not* for sale."

"Everything is for sale, sweetheart." His heart pounded so hard she could surely feel it through the folder.

She wrenched her hand out of his light grip. "And even if that were true, which it's not, Your Ride isn't worth a billion dollars."

"Sure it is."

She rolled her eyes in an exaggerated way, her chest heaving. Even angry, she was beautiful, and he wanted to keep her here for as long as possible.

"A business is worth whatever someone is willing to pay for it," he said, hoping she didn't take his statement as business advice. "And I'm willing to pay one billion dollars for Your Ride."

Tears gathered in her eyes and Esther's chin quivered. "Why?" Her voice sounded pinched and timid and nothing like the bold, powerful woman he'd fallen in love with. "Are you trying to take everything I have?"

"What? No." He peered at her, trying to understand what he'd done wrong. He knew how much Your Ride was worth, and it was a heck of a lot less than a billion dollars.

"Then why are you doing this?" She dropped her hands to her sides, the fight in her fading. At least this conversation had lasted long enough for that to happen.

"Why am I doing this?" He squinted at her, wishing he could see inside her mind. "Because I'm trying to get you back. I'm trying to apologize. I'm trying to tell you that I was wrong and shouldn't have—I should've trusted you more." His own chest heaved as his emotions came out of the box he'd stuffed them into.

Esther's gaze searched his, earnest and hopeful, but not quite believing. "How is buying my company a way to get me back?"

"Because it got you up here. It got you to come talk to me. And it could get you into the Nine-0 club, and we could be together, no secrets between us."

"Maybe you could've just called."

He scoffed. "Right. I know you better than that. Give me some credit."

"Your Ride still isn't for sell."

Marshall wanted to throw up his hands in defeat. He had no idea what to do now. Desperation clogged his throat and made his tongue thick.

The breeze kicked up, playing with her hair and telling him his time was almost up. She wouldn't stand on his front porch for much longer, and she wouldn't come in the house.

"Esther," he said, not even caring that all his feelings poured into the word. "Tell me what to do, and I'll do it." Marshall had always known what to do. This was a new feeling for him, and even as he stood waiting for her to respond, he knew he had to trust it. Trust her.

"I trust you," he said. "I love you. Tell me how to fix this."

Those tears appeared again, but she blinked them back. "I don't know, Marshall."

"You don't know what?"

She handed him the folder and fell back a step. She was about to leave and it took everything in him to stop himself from lunging forward and latching onto her hand so she'd stay just a little longer.

"I don't know if this can be fixed." She turned and went down the steps, this time much slower than her furious retreat yesterday. She paused at the driver's door and looked back at him. Their eyes met, and that same chemistry that had existed between them for the past couple of months was still there.

"It can be fixed," he called to her. "I'm going to fix it."

She nodded, but she still got in the car and drove away. And dang, if he'd pay every penny he had to make her stop doing that.

———

Monday found him scrambling around to get everything set for Fisher's return and proposal the following day. Marshall had gotten the ring bright and early, the gate buzzer actually interrupting his sprint on the treadmill.

He'd looked at the diamond, of course. It was huge, and beautiful, and made his chest collapse. He should've gotten back on the machine and put in another five miles, but he suddenly couldn't breathe.

He'd left the engagement ring on the front table and disappeared upstairs for a while, trying to brainstorm more ways to get Esther back in his life. If he called for a ride, he suspected she'd send another driver. His attempt to buy Your Ride had failed, not that he'd really wanted her business. He just wanted her.

Maybe that was all she needed to know. He pulled out his phone and sent her a text.

*I just want you. Hope you have a great day.*

She didn't respond, though he knew she'd be up by now. She was the most regimented and routined person he knew, something he actually loved about her. But she'd said he could just call or text, and while he didn't know how to get her back either, he wasn't going to stop trying.

He did get in touch with Tayla, and she snuck him into the gardens after the horticulturist at Aloha Hideaway had finished for the day.

Marshall stood in front of the row of flowers that Tayla indicated, no idea how to proceed. He could harvest pineapples and plant suckers and slips, dig a new drainage ditch and put bamboo in it. But cutting flowers to make a beautiful arrangement? Didn't people take classes for that kind of thing?

He looked at Tayla, a blonde woman who had to be a

decade younger than him. "Um. I don't quite know what I'm doing."

She smiled at him and handed him a pair of gloves. They didn't look anything like work gloves, but more like something that would protect the flowers from his hands, not the other way around.

"I'll cut," she said. "You hold. Now, Fisher said he wanted three big vases, so we'll probably need a few dozen flowers."

"Sure," Marshall said, though he had no idea how many flowers he'd need. Or how he'd hold a few dozen of them. But Tayla worked with strong, sure movements, and he simply took what she gave him.

After a few flowers, he said, "Are you dating anyone?"

She stilled for a moment before straightening and looking right at him. Her hospitable nature had fled completely. "Excuse me?"

"No, no," he said quickly. "I'm seeing someone. Well." He shrugged. "I've messed up, and I'm trying to get her back."

"Esther." Tayla cocked her hip, and Marshall should've known that everyone on the island would know about his relationship with his driver.

"Yes, Esther." He lifted his chin. "I'm taking any advice I can get. If your boyfriend had…done something you didn't like, how could he get you back?"

"What have you tried?"

Marshall didn't want to tell her, because his attempts had been ridiculous at best and he barely knew this woman. "Not much," he admitted.

She bent over and continued clipping blooms. "Don't you have a lot of money?"

Marshall accepted the flowers she handed back to him. "Sometimes."

She laughed and moved to the next row. "Right. I have money sometimes too."

"I don't think she can be bought." Esther was maybe one of the first women he'd known who couldn't. And he really liked that about her.

"Well, then do something besides throw your money around." She kept handing him flowers until she declared them done. Tayla instructed him to get them in water soon and to make sure the temperature in the room wasn't too warm.

Marshall did as instructed, setting up the vases in the appointed room and arranging the flowers to the best of his ability. He stood back to check his work, honestly unsure if anything he'd done that day was right.

Owen entered the room and stepped next to him. "Well, the vases look nice." He then proceeded to undo all of Marshall's work and make it look better.

"How do you know how to do this?" he asked.

"I run this hotel." Owen looked at him with a smile. "I'm a man of many talents."

"What are you and the boys doing tonight?"

"The boys are going to a movie on the fourth floor. I'm working."

"You work too much."

"We're at the height of the summer season, and Fisher's been gone for almost three weeks." Owen sounded a tad defensive, and Marshall couldn't blame him. He probably got told he worked too much by too many people.

"Want some company?"

"Only if you're going to keep your mouth shut so I can get the holiday bonuses done."

"Deal." After all, the last thing Marshall wanted to do was talk. Fish had texted a couple more times about Esther, and Marshall had conveniently ignored the messages. A measure of humiliation pulled through him when he thought of what he'd done by drawing up that ridiculous offer.

When Esther said she wasn't quite to nine zero status, she hadn't been kidding. And she was only about halfway there, which made his offer pretty ridiculous.

His phone buzzed, and when he saw Esther's name on the screen, his entire day improved.

*Thanks.*

A single word. Nothing more. But somehow it was the greatest text he'd ever received.

# SEVENTEEN

ESTHER STOOD in front of her bathroom mirror at five-fifteen on Tuesday morning, the puffiness around her eyes helpless. Everyone who looked at her would be able to see it, and she'd just put on her sunglasses and go to the beach like she had yesterday if she didn't have to play chauffeur for Fisher and Stacey.

He'd contacted her and asked her to help him with his surprise proposal. Esther had agreed, of course, but then she'd dug out a carton of ice cream and eaten in the hammock by herself, her feet trailing in the dirt as she tried to forget the things that had been said in that very spot.

She showered, brushed her teeth, put on her oils. She dressed, and styled her hair just so, and made her face look flawless with the help of some great cosmetics. By the time she finished her routine, she could've been the Esther that was psyching herself up to give one of her clients a birthday present.

Jaylani had taken Tuesdays and Thursdays off during the week, so Esther did all the morning driving on those days. And today, she'd scheduled a very important job at a fish taco stand. It was something quick, really. Just a man and his girlfriend as they went back to Sweet Breeze after lunch.

But she couldn't make the original pick-up at the airport. Stacey would know something was up if Esther was the one behind the wheel, and as her best friend had been right there for her since the break-up, Esther had arranged a sneaky bit of change-a-roo at the taco stand.

Another of her drivers was taking Stacey to the airport to meet Fisher, and Esther finished her morning jobs and got into position to switch with Fern, who normally only did night jobs. But she looked the most like Esther, with her short blond hair and slim figure.

Esther pulled into a parking lot one over from the taco stand and got out to walk. Everything ran like clockwork as she saw Fern coming toward her. The two women stopped in the middle of the sidewalk to exchange keys.

"Everything go okay?" Esther asked.

"Yep. They're getting food now. They should be ready in about fifteen minutes."

Esther looked down the beach to the line outside Old Sam's. The fisherman had hit it big when he'd decided to start his own restaurant instead of just selling to them. Judging by the popularity of the place, Fisher and Stacey would be at least fifteen minutes.

"Thanks, Fern. See you tonight."

The other woman went in the direction of Esther's car, and she continued down the pathway to find another sleek, black car parked in the public beach lot. Esther got behind the wheel and adjusted the air conditioning so it was blowing on her better.

With nothing else to do, she checked her phone. Another text from Marshall had come in earlier that morning, and she hadn't known how to respond. She tapped on his name, wishing she could get his brand off her heart. Then maybe his texts wouldn't burn so much.

*I miss you.*

She hadn't known how to respond. How could he say such things so openly? Why couldn't she let him know she felt the same way? Of course they wouldn't be spending every waking moment together, even if they did get married. But somehow the keen separation between them now was so palpable it made her whole body tense.

*I miss you too.* Esther had the words thumbed onto her screen when the back door opened. Fisher and Stacey had returned.

"Sweet Breeze, please," he said, and Esther eased the car out of the lot and headed toward the hotel. Stacey sighed into Fisher's side, and Esther tried not to watch them in the rearview mirror.

But she couldn't help it. Fisher leaned over and inhaled her hair, a stunningly romantic gesture that Esther longed for.

He whispered something to Stacey, who smiled and giggled a little. Esther pried her eyes away from them and focused on the road. Her grip on the wheel tightened until it was painful, and she set her jaw, willing herself not to cry.

Thankfully, she made it to the hotel without bursting into

tears, and Fisher kissed Stacey with all the slow passion of a man in love. Esther couldn't help reaching up to touch her own lips, remembering her own last, sweet kiss with Marshall. It had felt like that. Like drifting on a slow current, the cloudless blue sky above serene and perfect. Like falling in love. Like being loved.

Fisher got out of the car, and Stacey said, "Can you take me back to Aloha Hideaway, please?"

Esther knew she needed to give Fisher a few minutes to get up to the room. But she'd have to reveal herself to Stacey at some point. So she turned around and lowered her shades. "Hey, Stace."

Surprise crossed Stacey's face. "Esther. You're driving again?"

"A job's a job," she said. "As long as I don't have to drive Marshall around, I'm fine."

"What's your afternoon like?"

"Oh, nothing much." She tried to make her voice nonchalant and carefree. It sounded good to her own ears. "What about you?"

"I was thinking of going to the gardens, or maybe the beach. Should we text Tawny? See if she's gotten any closer to getting that surfer dude to ask her out?"

Esther saw her opening, and she seized onto it. "Sure. Want to run to your place and grab your stuff? Then we can come back here to change. I want to check my room for some earrings I lost, and then we'll go."

"Sounds great." Stacey slid over to the door and opened it. "Just a sec. I'm coming up front." Once her best friend was beside her, Esther drove the quick mile to Aloha Hideaway and stood under the swaying palms while Stacey ran inside to grab her beach things.

Then back at Sweet Breeze, Esther started to sweat. *Fifteen-twenty-one*, she chanted to herself, hoping Stacey wouldn't put up too much fuss about going to that room. Maybe she didn't even remember that was where she'd first stayed when she was spying on Fisher's hotel. Fisher had certainly remembered, and the room number had been drilled into Esther's head.

Every step took her and Stacey closer to the proposal, and every breath of Esther's became harder and harder. She wanted this so badly for herself, and while she didn't begrudge her best friend's happiness, it also burned like wildfire.

She nodded to Owen at the front desk, who met her eye, grinned, and then bent over his phone. He was to alert Fisher that the women were here, so he'd be ready inside the room. It seemed like they had to wait forever for an elevator, as an exceptionally large group had obviously just checked in. They filled two cars before Esther and Stacey could squeeze onto one.

"It's to the right," Esther said when Stacey stepped off before her. She waited at the corner, and Esther went first down the hall toward the appointed room. She put the key in the lock and waited for the green light and the beep before letting it crack a bit, giving Fisher just another clue that they'd arrived.

"You've been staying here since Saturday?"

"Yes. And I just need another set of eyes to find the earrings." Esther sounded like she really had lost a pair of earrings, and she was proud of her performance. If Stacey or Fisher knew how big of a toll this charade was taking on her, they'd feel bad. So she stuck on her happy face, and pushed the door open. "They're my seashell ones."

"The seashell ones," Stacey said. "Got it." She went inside, but Esther loitered in the doorway. The room was beautiful, with vases of Stacey's unique navy-purple hibiscus flowers—and Fisher, looking dapper and every inch the billionaire he was in that fancy suit.

Stacey froze and said, "What—?" before her eyes roamed the room. She looked back at Fisher. "Fisher?"

"Stacey," he said, the word bobbling in his throat a little. Esther enjoyed watching him interact when he was nervous, because it made him more human. And he loved Stacey so much, it was almost sickening.

"I'm in love with you, and I don't want to wait to make you my wife. I know it's fast, but sometimes when two people fall in love, it happens quickly." He flicked his eyes to Esther, who heard the power and truth in his statement.

She'd fallen in love with Marshall just by driving him from his home to work and back each day. Once they'd started dating, all those feelings had simply been cemented by how good he was, how kind, how hardworking.

Fisher dropped to one knee and opened the little black box he held. "Will you marry me?"

Stacey shifted her feet and pressed one hand to her chest. "Fisher."

Esther almost rolled her eyes at her best friend's warning tone. Did she think he was joking? Esther herself had gone to too much work for this to be a prank. She stepped further into the room and nudged Stacey forward. "Go on."

"Are you serious?" Stacey asked.

"I'm not down on one knee for fun." Fisher looked like he was about to throw up, and Esther's patience was waning too. Could Stacey not *see* how much Fisher adored her?

Dropping to the floor she took his hand holding the ring box in both of hers. She snapped the lid closed after looking at the diamond for only a moment. "Yes." She laughed, tears streaming down her face.

"Yeah?" Fisher asked.

Stacey nodded, smiling and crying and trembling. "Yeah."

His face exploded into a grin. "I love you." He bent forward and kissed her. "I want you to be mine."

"I love you, too, Fisher."

He opened the box again and slipped the ring on Stacey's finger, and Esther's whole world came to a screeching halt. Everything she'd just witnessed was amazing. Two people that loved each other were making a commitment to each other. Had Fisher done everything perfect? No. Had Stacey? Certainly not. But they'd found their way through their issues and problems together.

*Together.*

Esther didn't want to be alone anymore. She wanted a diamond of her own. A billionaire of her own. And she was the only one standing in her way.

She turned and fled down the hall, her heart trying to leap out of her chest. Jabbing at the call button, a set of tears threatened to ruin her flawless face. She wasn't sure she cared.

She simply needed to get to Marshall right now.

Stepping into the car, she fumbled to get her phone out of her pocket. She still hadn't sent him the text, and she hastily thumbed it off, choosing to send *Where are you right now?* instead.

On a Tuesday at just after lunch, Esther could make some guesses. She ran through the lobby, her heels clacking against the tile, realizing she'd have to wait for her car from the valet.

She handed Sterling the ticket, and said, "Can you please hurry?"

"For you, Esther, anything." He beamed at her, and handed the ticket to another attendant. It seemed like forever but was probably less than five minutes before her car pulled up in the drive.

"Thanks." She got behind the wheel, anxious that Marshall hadn't answered her yet. "So the office," she said, setting the car toward the plantation on the north side of the island. She didn't bother to pull into a proper parking spot. She barely had the wherewithal to take the keys out of the ignition.

She arrived outside his office out of breath, having run up the three flights of stairs. The windows were dark. He wasn't here. She spun back toward the room and asked the first woman she saw, "Has Mister Robison been in today?"

"No, ma'am. We haven't seen him." The brunette smiled and went back to her computer, leaving Esther with only one place to go: his house.

Once through the coded gate and standing on his front porch, she pounded on the door. He didn't answer for several long seconds. "Marshall!" she called like she had last time she'd been here to confront him about his offer on Your Ride. "Are you home?"

She banged again, but he still didn't come. He hadn't answered her text.

She moved around the side of the house to the patio that overlooked the beach. The sound of distant waves crashing against the rocks met her ears, as did the soft sound of a cat's meow. Turning back to the house, she found a gray cat sitting on the windowsill, watching her.

Marshall didn't own a cat. So how did that feline get inside?

Esther stepped over to the French doors and reached for the handle, sure Marshall kept everything locked up tight. But the handle went down easily, and she stepped right inside his house as the cat streaked out.

It felt like a tomb, and it was obvious that he hadn't been here in a few days. She hadn't been able to go home either, so she understood. Standing in his kitchen, she searched for where he could be.

*Sweet Breeze.* She could figure that out by simply calling Owen and asking if Marshall was a registered guest at the hotel. So she did. And he wasn't.

*His boat.*

With a shout of triumph, Esther left the way she came in and hurried back to her car. Hopefully, he was on land, but as she drove down the twisty mountain roads and to the docks, her mind whispered that he probably wasn't, that him being way out on the ocean waters was probably why he still hadn't answered her text.

Sure enough, when she parked at the docks, it was next to a Robison Plantation SUV. His boat wasn't tied in its usual place, so Esther walked across the wooden planks and sat down, hoping with everything in her that he wouldn't stay out on the water past nightfall.

# EIGHTEEN

MARSHALL PILOTED the catamaran back toward shore, hoping he beat the setting of the sun. He could grab some dinner and more groceries and sleep on the boat tied to the dock. But he didn't like trying to navigate into his spot without being able to see.

As his phone came back into cell range, it blinged a whole slew of times. One name made his breath catch in his throat.

Esther.

*Where are you right now?*

It was impossible for him to know when she'd sent the message. The timestamp said nine-twenty-four, the time it was now. He'd been out on the boat since putting the flowers in the room for Fisher that morning. He'd placed the ring box exactly where his friend had told him to, and then he'd gone out onto the water, needing the peace and calmness being away from everything provided.

His office manager had texted several times, as had Fisher.

But it was only Esther who mattered to him. Instead of texting her back, he tapped the phone icon and placed a call. The dock loomed closer, the masts of other boats puncturing the sunset sky of orange, pink, gold, and navy blue.

The line rang against his ear, but he also heard the shrill *riiiiing!* bounce off the water in front of him.

"Where are you?" she demanded.

So she was still mad, and Marshall sighed. "I spent the day on the ocean. I'm coming in now."

She exhaled into the phone, one long sigh that alerted Marshall to the fact that maybe she wasn't angry with him anymore. "Oh, okay. So I'll see you in a second."

"You're at the dock?"

"Yes."

"Why?"

She didn't answer immediately, and Marshall searched the horizon for her though he was still a bit too far out to see her. Only two minutes later, though, he saw her silhouette against the bright sky, and he wanted to throw the throttle into its highest gear.

He didn't, exercising control as he maneuvered the craft in delicately, and taking the time to tie the boat off securely. Then he stepped onto the dock to face her.

"I can't believe you're here," he said, giving away every-thing he'd been trying to dump in the ocean these past few days. "What's going on?" He glanced around and found evidence that she'd been sitting on the dock for a while. A white takeout bag sat there, the top open.

"I...I love you," she blurted out. In the next moment, she clapped her palm over her mouth as her eyes went wide.

Marshall couldn't help the smile that crept across his mouth, even if he didn't understand what was going on. "I already like this conversation more than the previous two we've had."

Esther lowered her hand, her eyes glinting but whether it was with frustration or flirtation, Marshall still wasn't sure. "I don't like what you did, but I think I...understand why you did it."

"I've never claimed to be perfect." *She* had put that label on him, and it was better she know now that he made mistakes. "I'm sorry for not trusting you."

"Do you trust me now?"

Marshall cocked his head and folded his arms. "Depends on what's in that takeout bag."

"Oh, did you not eat dinner?" Her tone reeked of flirtation now. "Sorry, I ate the double bacon cheeseburger while I waited for you to come in."

Marshall laughed, beyond thrilled when Esther joined him and then flung herself into his arms. He caught her around the waist and spun with her, leaning his forehead down until he touched hers. "I'm so glad you're here."

She closed her eyes and held onto his shoulders. "I was watching Fisher propose to Stacey, and I realized the only person keeping me away from you was me."

"I won't look into your private business again," he promised. "I don't know why I did it. Well, I did. I just... you'd been driving me for years, and I was worried that maybe your business was in trouble and you were being extra-nice to me because you needed money."

"I've had a crush on you for years," she whispered, her mouth inching closer to his. "That's all I've ever wanted from you, Marshall. This." She pressed into him. "Us."

"Us," he repeated, really liking the sound of that. He watched her for an extra moment, the happy glow on her face reaching out and touching his heart. Lowering his head further, he touched his mouth to hers, glad when she sighed and kissed him like she really did love him.

————

The next morning, Marshall woke to the sound of Esther calling his name. He forced himself to keep his eyes closed even as he became aware of her lavender scent and her footfalls as she came closer.

"Marshall," she whispered. Her delicate hand touched his shoulder and he let his eyes drift open to behold the stunning beauty of her face only a few inches from his.

"Hey, love." He reached up and brushed her hair out of her face, liking the way she leaned into his touch and smiled softly.

"I can't believe you're still asleep."

He pushed himself up to sitting, noticing the way the bright morning sunshine came through the skylights. "No? What time is it? Six instead of five?"

She gave a half laugh, half scoff. "It's almost seven-thirty."

Marshall yawned, surprised himself at how long he'd slept. "I guess I haven't been getting too much rest lately."

Something flashed across her face, but she erased it quickly. "Well, come on. You told me I could drive you today, and I've been sitting in the car for thirty minutes."

"Probably forty," he said. "The Esther I know shows up ten minutes early."

She gave him a flirty, daggered look and fell back a couple of steps. "Maybe I'm not the Esther you know."

She definitely wasn't wearing her usual chauffeur clothes, but a bright pink dress without straps, leaving her shoulders exposed and the curve of her chest the only thing keeping the dress from falling off.

Marshall hastily brought his eyes back to hers. "Yep. Looks like the Esther I know." Or the one he really wanted to know. "Are we not working today?"

"I'll take you if you want, but you said you'd buy me breakfast on the beach."

"Ah, yes I did." He threw the comforter off his legs and stood, his head almost touching the ceiling in the cabin. "Well, let's go."

Her face reddened, and she backed toward the door again. "I'll let you get dressed." She made a hasty retreat, and Marshall looked down at his bare chest and athletic shorts. A chuckle started in his chest and continued while he changed into a pair of shorts and a polo. That was proper beach breakfast attire, wasn't it?

He joined Esther on the dock and they walked to the car hand in hand. "Are you still staying at Sweet Breeze?" he asked.

"How did you know I was there?"

"Owen told me." He couldn't tell if that information bothered her or not. Didn't seem to.

"No, I went home last night after I left here."

She meant after he apologized three more times and after they made out on the boat a little. His body heated just thinking about it.

"When are you going home?" she asked.

Marshall looked up to the cliffs, as if he could see his house from here. "I don't know." He sighed a mighty sigh. "I'm thinking of selling my place and getting something a little smaller. Somewhere closer to town."

"Really?" Esther paused near the passenger door and trained her blue eyes on him. He lost himself to her, just like he had dozens of times before.

"Mm hm." He gathered her into his arms and kissed her. "Maybe somewhere by this cute little beach bungalow I visit from time to time. I saw a place near there that was for sale."

She pushed on his chest and searched his eyes. "The Martin farm?"

"Is it a farm?"

"That's the only place by me that's for sale."

"Well, I don't really want a farm. Is it chickens and stuff?"

Esther giggled. "I'd like to see you and a chicken together in the same yard." She laughed now, the sound catapulting up to the sky. She turned and opened the door, sliding into the passenger seat and leaving the door open.

"So I guess I'm driving." He closed the door to more laughter and went around to get behind the wheel. "But really, what kind of farm?" Maybe he could have a pineapple plantation down near the beach.

"Macadamia nuts," she said. "It's small, I think only five hundred acres or so. All hand worked. The Martin's are retiring, and they don't have children."

A pit opened in Marshall's stomach. He could find himself in that exact situation in only a decade or so. And he didn't need another crop to take care of. He could figure out how to cultivate, harvest, and sell macadamia nuts if he had to. But he didn't have to, and he said, "Well, I'll keep looking then."

He pulled onto the street and headed toward the coffee house where she got their drinks each morning. As he put on his signal to turn left, she said, "No, go right here."

"Right?" He glanced in that direction. "But The Roast is to the left."

"Coffee is not breakfast."

"Uh…yes it is. It's all we ever have for breakfast. I literally don't think I've see you ever eat in the morning."

"I eat." She sounded a bit wounded.

"I mean, obviously you eat," he said. "But not even a banana for breakfast."

"Today, I want to eat breakfast."

Marshall glanced at her, surprised by the bite in her tone and the set of her jaw. "All right. It's fine. You want to go right, let's go right." He swung the car in that direction, thinking it would probably be easier if she just told him where she wanted him to go.

But she didn't. She sat on her hands and directed him only moments before he was supposed to make a turn.

Somehow they ended up at her bungalow, and he didn't even know how he'd gotten there.

"Yeah, so I don't think I should drive again," he said. "You're so much better at it than I am." He killed the engine and looked at her, hoping his tone had been playful enough.

Esther looked like she was going to throw up, and she got out of the car without responding to his jest. He followed her, wondering why she'd come to the docks in that pink dress if they were just going to come back to her place. And he had no hope of actually eating anything here, as Esther had claimed not to be skilled in the kitchen.

"Where are we going?" he called after her as she bent to retrieve something from the porch.

"The beach." She shouldered her bag and extended her hand for him to take.

He grabbed onto her and said, "You and the beach."

"I love the beach."

"I know you do." She'd told him something about how it grounded her, how she felt connected to the earth when she was on the beach, like her life was more than driving tourists and billionaires around. He was happy she liked the beach, no matter the reason, just like he enjoyed the way she smelled but didn't really believe in the healing properties of peppermint oil.

He went with her through the copse of trees, emerging onto a beautiful beach with pristine, blue water. "Wow, this is beautiful."

She paused and got out a towel, spreading it on the sand. Marshall gazed out at the water, peace flowing through him the way the island breeze chased itself around the island.

"So I have to ask you something."

He turned to find her concealing something behind her back. His interest piqued, he narrowed his eyes as his pulse picked up. "You have to ask me something?"

Esther nodded, her expression grave. "How traditional are you?"

Marshall had no idea how to answer. "In what way?"

She brought her hands out from behind her back, but he couldn't see anything. "I have my great-grandmother's wedding ring. I was thinking if we got engaged, that would be the ring I'd want to wear." Esther held up a simple gold band, with a simple diamond set on it.

Before he could say a word, she stepped closer, her eyes earnest, filled with that eternal hope that he loved. "Marshall, will you marry me?"

His eyebrows shot up. "You're asking me to marry you?" Panic and hope and love and frustration coiled through him. This wasn't how things were supposed to go. This couldn't be the story told for generations to come. Could it?

"Yes, and forego the diamond shopping." She looked down at her ring and then started to slip it on her finger.

Marshall practically knocked the diamond out of her hand in his haste to stop her from putting her own engagement ring on her own finger. "Esther." Slight exasperation filled the word.

"What?" She gazed up at him, searching his face. "Oh, you're traditional."

"I would like to be the one to ask." He spoke as gently as he could, hoping she'd feel and hear his love for her.

She handed him the ring and settled her weight on her back foot.

"Oh, you mean right now." Marshall looked down at the ring and then back to Esther.

She cocked one eyebrow. "I already asked you and you didn't even answer."

He fiddled with the ring, turning it over and over. "Esther, I love you. I love you when I didn't think it was possible to fall in love again." A smile touched his lips, crinkling his eyes. He looked at her, glad when he found her eyes filled with tears and her chin doing that adorable quiver.

"Will you marry me?" He dropped to both knees in front of her, the sand hotter than he was expecting, and held her great-grandmother's ring up as if she'd never seen it before.

She considered him for a moment before her face broke into a grin. "Yes. Yes, I'll marry you."

He laughed as he stood, slid the ring on her finger, and kissed her. And this slow, sweet kiss with his fiancée was better than Marshall could've ever hoped to have in his life again.

---

Read on for a sneak peek at **WOMEN'S BEACH CLUB**, the next book in the Getaway Bay Resort Romance series.

# SNEAK PEEK! WOMEN'S BEACH CLUB CHAPTER ONE

TYLER RIGBY PUSHED his foot against the ground, giving his hammock another gentle sway. The afternoon hours were some of the longest, and while he should've been used to them after six years, he still wasn't.

It was moments like this that he thought maybe he should get a job. The idea only stayed for a breath, a fleeting moment. But it had been plaguing him for a few months now.

"Maybe after Christmas," he said to the golden retriever. "Yeah, Lazy Bones?" He pushed the hammock again. "Maybe after Christmas." Which was still a couple of months away too.

Not that Tyler kept track of time anymore. He had no reason to, other than he liked eating eggs for breakfast and going somewhere for dinner. And no one had their dinner menu on at three o'clock in the afternoon.

The waves of the bay lapped at the shore a hundred

yards away, and Tyler focused on them as his phone buzzed against his bare chest.

His brother, Wayne, who still lived in New York City, still ran the multi-billion-dollar online poker company they'd founded together almost a decade ago, still kept in touch on a daily basis.

Tyler had trained his brother not to talk to him about poker, the company, or anything business related. He had financial advisors for that, and speaking with them quarterly was horrific enough.

Wayne's message was a picture of him and his two kids, and it said, *It's Darius's birthday* underneath it.

Tyler snapped to attention. One thing about having a huge fortune at his disposal and countless hours on his hands was that he sometimes forgot what day it was. Darius was one of only two nephews, and the boy would only turn six once.

So Tyler called the toy store in New York City, and got someone to deliver a set of the toy cars his nephew liked so much. That done, he decided he could head inside his modest home and get ready for dinner.

After all, he hadn't showered yet, believing the best hours for showering were between three and five p.m. As he stepped out of the bathtub in his one bedroom house on the beach, something clunked and then a soft scrape followed.

The mail. He looked forward to the mail every day, as it simply gave him something to look forward to. He'd thought more and more often lately that if he had a girl-friend, he'd have something else—something fun—to anticipate.

He wrapped a towel around his waist and went to collect that day's excitement. He thumbed through the envelopes, finally pulling a cream-colored one out of the stack. It had elegant script on the front, reading *Mister Tyler Rigby* and ending with his beachside address on Getaway Bay.

He opened the letter, wondering what it could be. Probably another invitation to some fundraiser. Though he wanted to maintain a low profile on the big island of Hawaii, everyone seemed to know he was loaded.

He pulled out an equally eggshell-colored piece of paper, already dreading what it said on it. His attention perked up when he realized it was an invitation to the gala celebrating the completion of the new children's wing of the Bay Hospital. Since he'd made a sizable donation—really, without him, the wing wouldn't have been possible—he and a guest were invited to the fancy-pants dinner next weekend.

*Something else to look forward to.* As soon as he thought it, he tossed the pages to the kitchen counter. He'd be expected to take someone. The last ritzy dinner party he'd attended alone, he'd gotten quite the tongue-lashing from the media.

Problem was, he didn't have a significant other. He hadn't done it to hurt anyone, show anyone up, or boast about his wealth, as the article had claimed.

Lazy Bones whined, and Tyler went to work filling the dog's water bowl and dishing up more dog food. With the retriever lapping at the water, Tyler snatched his phone from the counter. Within seconds, he had Marshall Robison on the line.

"Dude, I need a date to a charity event," he said.

"I'm not really your type," Marshall said.

Tyler could practically see him bent over a stack of paper-work at his desk. Marshall owned the largest pineapple plantation on the island, and they were both members of the Hawaii Nine-0 club, an informal organization for the men and women who had nine zeroes in their bank accounts.

"Very funny," Tyler said. "I'm just wondering...you used to have a lot of different women go to events with you. Where...well, where did you find them?"

"Oh, that's easy," Marshall said. "You just ask someone you already know. Tell them explicitly that you're not looking for a relationship. It's not a date. You'll buy them a fancy dress, and they'll hang on your arm, and get a free meal, and pose for the pictures. Most women like that."

Tyler couldn't think of a single person he knew who even wanted a fancy dress. Or knew how to pose.

"Want me to set you up with someone?" Marshall asked.

That idea was even more horrifying than going alone. He'd be spending hours with this woman, and he'd like to be able to enjoy the money he spent, maybe have a decent conversation. Okay, so maybe he should just be looking for someone to ask. If they wanted to think it was a date, well, would that be so bad?

Only one person came to mind, and he wasn't sure if she'd even remember him. He hadn't spoken to her in months, and he was surprised the beach yoga instructor hadn't called the police on him for stalking with a dog. Could he help it if Lazy Bones liked her stretch of the beach the best? Could he help it if he liked watching her hold diffi-cult yoga poses with ease?

No, he couldn't help either of those things.

"Ty?" Marshall asked.

No matter how many times Tyler had told Marshall not to call him that, he still did. The man had a fixation on nicknames.

"I'm good," Tyler said. "Thanks, *Marsh*." He hung up, a low chuckle in the back of his throat. When he came out of the bedroom after getting dressed, Lazy Bones stood by the back door, a Frisbee hanging loosely in his mouth.

"You want to go throw?" Tyler took the toy from his dog and headed back out to the beach. If there was one thing he loved doing to occupy all his free time, it was working with, training, and playing with Lazy Bones.

His feet drank up the warmth in the sand, though it wasn't as hot in October as it was over the summer. As he completed the easy motions of throwing the Frisbee and treating Bones, his mind ran through possible ways to approach the beautiful yoga instructor and not make a fool of himself.

An hour later, he still didn't have any good ideas, but it was close enough to dinnertime to wander down the beach and find something to eat. He rounded the curve in the beach and drank in the sight of Getaway Bay before him.

At the pinnacle of the bay sat Sweet Breeze, the luxury hotel that had just celebrated its one-year anniversary. Fisher DuPont owned and operated the hotel, and he was also a member of the Hawaii Nine-0 club.

Several stands and huts dotted the bay, and he could get tacos, fruity drinks or sodas, fish sandwiches, anything with spam on it, popcorn, and the best grilled pineapple on the island right here. Tyler loved eating on the beach, and while he sometimes wondered what he was doing with his life, he loved living the way he did.

After so many years in the spotlight, with the designer suits, and the fancy haircuts, and never being able to leave the house without a security detail, he'd come to Hawaii—to Getaway Bay—to well, get away.

He didn't own more than one suit now, and most days he didn't even put on shirt.

His eyes wandered down the beach, to the dozens of vacationers in Sweet Breeze's private beach—and his gaze stalled.

The cute yoga instructor with brown hair streaked with blonde was conducting class.

He'd met her over the summer, and yeah, he'd thought her fit and fun and probably fabulous. He wasn't really sure, as he'd never worked up the courage to talk to her past saying, "Sorry about that," when Bones had knocked his Frisbee into the woman's beach yoga class. He'd never even gotten her name.

Perhaps it was time to do exactly that.

With new purpose in his stride, he stopped at the seafood stand first and Two Coconuts, the drink hut, second. Properly fed and hydrated, he approached the yoga class, which was just getting out. He'd seen the woman plenty of times, and he'd seen the cup from Two Coconuts by her mat as well. He carried a second one with him, having done a bit of espionage at the drink stand.

He stopped several feet away and watched as she toweled herself off. She had well-defined muscles in her arms and legs, a trim waist, and all the right curves in all the right places.

She caught his eye and froze. Tyler lifted the cup in what he hoped was a universal gesture of *I got this for you so you'll go to a fancy event with me next weekend, and hey, I'll buy you a dress if you don't have one.*

She actually glanced over her shoulder, as if she expected someone else to be standing there. Someone else he wanted to talk to. A pin of guilt pricked his heart. His many hours at the poker table had taught him to read people really well. Sometimes it was actually a curse, because he instinctively knew he'd hurt this woman by not talking to her when he should have.

She took a tentative step toward him, and he moved too. "Hey," he said. "So, uh, I'm Tyler." He extended the drink toward her.

She lifted the one she already had, and a wall of foolishness hit him. "I know who you are," she said, a note of disdain in her voice.

"Oh, yeah?"

"Yeah." He lifted the drink to his own lips and sucked. Pure sugar coated his mouth, and he spat the offending liquid out. It stained the sand blue, and he stared at it in horror. "What is this stuff?"

"Blue raspberry," she said, cocking one hip in a way that made his heart pound a little faster. And not because he was striking out and wouldn't have a date to the gala. But because, as he had for months, he found her so, so attractive.

That smattering of freckles on her face. The streaks of

blonde in her light brown hair. Those blue-green eyes, the same color as the bay.

Lazy Bones trotted right up to her and began to sniff in all the wrong places. Tyler tried to get between the two of them. "Bones," he chastised. "Stop it."

"Oh, he's fine." She bent and patted Lazy Bones, the smile on her face the first genuine gesture he'd seen since approaching. Bones soaked up the attention as if Tyler never gave the dog a good scrub. He grinned at the woman as if telling Tyler he'd been knocking his Frisbee in to this woman's yoga class for a reason.

"What's your name?" he asked.

She straightened, and Lazy Bones went back to the sniffing. Her eyes blazed, and for one, two, three terrible moments, he thought she'd stalk off. Instead she asked, "Did you ask Mo at the drink stand what I like?"

She'd find out anyway, so Tyler said, "No. Her name was Leilani."

"Why?"

"I have—I want—I *need* a date." He was so rusty when it came to women, he might as well leave now. Send in his own scathing article to the paper and take a selfie of him shirtless and unshowered for the photo. He tried to get Bones away from her, though he thought she smelled pretty amazing too. Like suntan lotion, and sand, and sun, and sweat.

"Is that an invitation to go out with you?" She plucked the drink cup from his hand and removed the straw. She handed it back to him and put her straw in before taking a great big drink. She finished with a long, "Ahhhh, that's good," and a cocked eyebrow.

He stared at her and then started laughing. "Okay, I deserve that."

"You really do." She made no move to give him the drink back. No problem. He'd bought it for her.

"So I donated a bunch of money to the children's wing at the hospital, and they're having their celebratory gala." Tyler watched her for any tells, anything that would indicate how she felt about what he was saying. She remained wooden, her emotions carefully hidden behind a mask. She'd be very good at poker.

"It'll be boring, and it's a black tie event," he continued. "*Very* stuffy. Very non-yoga. But I'm wondering if maybe you'd like to come with me."

He put on his poker face too, and though it was out of practice, it allowed him to make it through several seconds of silence. Was she ever going to answer?

He cocked his hip too. Two could play this game, and he was pretty sure his time at a poker table meant he could outwait her.

———

Read **WOMEN'S BEACH CLUB** today! It's a clean and wholesome sweet beach read, with plenty of sunshine, mysteries, and a fake relationship!

# BOOKS IN THE GETAWAY BAY® RESORT ROMANCE SERIES

**Aloha Hideaway Inn (Book 1):** Can Stacey and the Aloha Hideaway Inn survive strange summer weather, the arrival of the new resort, *and* the start of a special relationship?

**Getaway Bay (Book 2):** Can Esther deal with dozens of business tasks, unhappy tourists, *and* the twists and turns in her new relationship?

**Women's Beach Club (Book 3):** With the help of her friends in the Beach Club, can Tawny solve the mystery, stay safe, and keep her man?

**Straw and Diamonds (Book 4):** Can Sasha maintain her sanity amidst their busy schedules, her issues with men like Jasper, and her desires to take her business to the next level?

**The Billionaire Club (Book 5):** Can Lexie keep her business affairs in the shadows while she brings her relationship out of them? Or will she have to confess everything to her new friends...and Jason?

**Sweet Breeze Resort (Book 6):** Can Gina manage her business across the sea and finish the remodel at Sweet Breeze, all while developing a meaningful relationship with Owen and his sons?

**Rainforest Retreat (Book 7):** As their paths continue to cross and Lawrence and Maizee spend more and more time together, will he find in her a retreat from all the family pressure? Can Maizee manage her relationship with her boss, or will she once again put her heart—and her job—on the line?

**Getaway Bay Singles (Book 8):** Can Katie bring him into her life, her daughter's life, and manage her business while he manages the app? Or will everything fall apart for a second time?

Turn the page to view series starters from three of my other series!

# BOOKS IN THE GETAWAY BAY® ROMANCE SERIES

Escape to Getaway Bay and meet your new best friends as these women navigate their careers, their love lives, and their own dreams and desires. Each heartwarming love story shows the power of women in their own lives and the lives of their friends.

**The Island House (Book 1):** Charlotte Madsen's whole world came crashing down six months ago with the words, "I met someone else."

**Can Charlotte navigate the healing process to find love again?**

# BOOKS IN THE STRANDED IN GETAWAY BAY® ROMANCE SERIES

Meet the McLaughlin Sisters in Getaway Bay as they encounter disaster after disaster...including the men they get stranded with. From ex-boyfriends to cowboys to football stars, these sisters can bring any man to his knees when the cards are stacked against them.

**The Perfect Storm (Book 1):** A freak storm has her sliding down the mountain...right into the arms of her ex. As Eden and Holden spend time out in the wilds of Hawaii trying to survive, their old flame is rekindled. But with secrets and old feelings in the way, will Holden be able to take all the broken pieces of his life and put them back together in a way that makes sense? Or will he lose his heart and the reputation of his company because of a single landslide?

# BOOKS IN THE CARTER'S COVE ROMANCE SERIES

Visit the South Carolina coast and The Heartwood Inn in these clean and wholesome beach romances. Each romance features a Heartwood sister navigating the potholes of romance with someone they DEFINITELY don't get along with...

**The Heartwood Sea (Book 1):** She owns The Heartwood Inn. He needs the land the inn sits on to impress his boss. Neither one of them will give an inch. But will they give each other their hearts?

# ABOUT ELANA

Elana Johnson is the USA Today bestselling and Kindle All-Star author of dozens of clean and wholesome contemporary romance novels. She lives in Utah, where she mothers two fur babies, works with her husband full-time, and eats a lot of veggies while writing. Find her on her website at authorelanajohnson.com